For Geoff, L...

THE
12-DAY
JINX

Love & bestwishes
Maith, Linda
&
Eleanor
XX
X

THE 12-DAY JINX

Mark Roberts

Andersen Press • London

For Edna, Linda and Eleanor
Three generations, three graces

First published in 2002 by
Andersen Press Limited,
20 Vauxhall Bridge Road, London SW1V 2SA
www.andersenpress.co.uk

British Library Cataloguing in Publication Data available
ISBN 1 84270 074 X

Typeset by FiSH Books, London WC1
Printed and bound in Great Britain by Mackays of Chatham Ltd., Chatham, Kent

MONDAY 2nd FEBRUARY

Chapter 1

It was turning out to be the best day ever.

Overnight, a heavy snow had started falling, covering everything it touched four fingers thick in a crisp white blanket.

And it only stopped falling as we turned the last corner of our journey and hit the deserted school gates. No boys or girls, no mums or dads, no prams or cars, it could only mean one thing. I thought Dirk, my unidentical twin (a boy, a member of the opposite sex, almost twice as tall but half as bright as me), was going to fly. He leapt with delight, hung in the air for a half-second like a weird bird and came down on the snowbound pavement with a rib-rattling roar of happiness. Together we danced in front of the gates, skidding and sliding by the notice that told us:

SCHOOL CLOSED TODAY
DUE TO FOUL WEATHER

MR M. SPANNER. HEAD TEACHER.

The first floor library window flew open as we sent a hail of snowballs at Isis, the caretaker's beady blue-eyed Siamese cat, and Spanner stuck his balding head out. The great long tuft of hair, usually drawn across the Head Teacher's skull to disguise the fact that his head was as bare as a newborn baby's bum, flapped in the February breeze like the national flag of Baldiland.

'Ellie! Dirk! Leave Mr Slater's cat alone! Didn't you hear the announcement on the radio? Snow! School closed! Now go home!'

He slammed the window shut and a heap of snow dropped from the roof, splatting down on Isis and burying her alive in the click of a clack of a fast pair of fingers.

'Come on, Dirk,' I said. 'Let's go to town!'

'Hang on, Ellie!' he called, as he rushed across the yard and started to dig Isis out with his bare hands.

'Oh, Dirk!' I called. 'She's a flaming cat, she's got nine lives, eight more than us. She'll outlive you and me. Leave her to it. The snow'll melt before she suffocates.'

But, as usual, he wasn't listening. He just went right on tossing bundles of snow over his shoulders and making friendly cat noises to calm her down. Howling and yowling, Isis bounced out of the mini-avalanche as Dirk screamed and held his hand up to show me she'd scratched him after he'd taken the trouble to rescue her.

'Why'd she do that?' His bottom lip was wobbling and tears were forming in his eyes, as I wrapped the last of my Handi-Andies around the scratch and clapped a hand on his shoulder. 'Because she doesn't know any better, Dirk. Because she's a cat. Because she was scared, I suppose.'

'S'ppose so!' he snuffled.

'Hey, Dirkie Turkey!' I ran off down the pavement. 'Race you into town!'

He brightened up, like the lights had just been turned on inside his head, and hared down the street after me.

'Don't call me Dirkie Turkey,' he laughed.

'OK, Dirk the Jerk, then!'

He laughed as we raced to the end of the road, and down the hill towards the town, down to the sea where all the shops were. Dirk screamed with delight and made a noise like a car alarm, waking up anyone in the neighbourhood who might still have been sleeping.

Chapter 2

CLOSED DUE TO BAD WEATHER.

Our town, Hexhill-on-Sea was shut. The whole of the rotten, stinking, good-for-nothing seaside town was closed due to bad weather.

Mick's Café, where we were welcome, closed. Las Vegas Gaming Arcade, where we weren't welcome, closed. The Ritzy Video Shop, closed. Planet X Comic Market, closed. Cyberspace Internet Café, closed. Doran's Department Store, possibly the most boring place in the universe, open.

Between us, we had bus fare, but the buses weren't running because of the snow, so we had some money. All 74p of it. We took a blind run at Doran's revolving doors, past the lipsticks and perfumes, through the knickers and bras, up the escalator, beyond the carpets and sofas, around the paints and plants, and up a last flight of stairs to the empty café on the top floor, where we bought a pot of tea for one (70p), and asked for two cups, which we took to a window seat overlooking the beach and the sea and the cliffs.

Dirk jangled the 4p change in his hands and told me, 'It's stopped snowing!'

'I know,' I said, staring outside. Boredom was already nibbling at me.

'What are we gonna do, Ellie?' he asked, throwing all

the money we owned down. 'I mean, what can we do 'cos we've got no money and even if we did have everything's closed and...' As he spoke, a light must've gone on inside his head. He raised his hands and wriggled his fingers, seeking out the words to explain his brilliant idea. 'I know, Ellie!' His voice echoed round the empty spaces, stuck on some words like he did when he was excited. 'Let's get a, get a, get a sledge and go sleighing down the sand dunes!'

I eyed my twin. He came first in the good looks department, he was even older than me − by a clear minute and a half. But he was as thick as a barrowful of broken bricks.

'Dirk,' I reminded him. 'We haven't got a sledge, matey. And we haven't got sledge money.'

'Well, I wish we did. I wish we had a sledge that went so fast it made you think you were flying. In fact, I wish I could fly!'

Fly? Now that we'd bought a pot of tea we didn't even have the money for a bus ride.

'I hate it here,' he groaned. 'It's boring!' Dirk's head dropped to the table. 'Nothing ever happens and nothing ever will!' He was banging the table with his forehead and moaning.

'Don't do that, Dirk!' I said, shaking him.

And it was at that very moment in time that I saw it, through the corner of my eye. And when I saw it, I gasped. I stood up to get a better look through the window, both eyes full on. 'Well, take a look at that!'

It appeared from nowhere. It glided along the road

from the beach straight towards the main street of the town, directly below us.

It was a white stretch limousine, with blacked-out windows and a TV aerial on the roof. It seemed to go on and on, all the way down each block it crossed as it carefully cut its way through the ice and the snow, cruising the town like a visiting spaceship and slowing down to a halt at the traffic lights outside Doran's Department Store.

'We must follow, follow, follow!' Dirk was on his feet and burning the rubber soles of his Reeboks, faster than a cat with a scorched bottom and I was directly after him. We jumped into the lift and were out through the revolving front doors in under a minute.

'I've just gotta, gotta, gotta, getta, getta, getta closer look!' Dirk sounded like a machine gun that was emptying all its bullets out in one short, sharp blast.

But when we exploded onto the pavement, the limo was gone and the only sign of it was a pair of tyre treads that ran down the block and round the corner. I pointed at the deep grooves in the snow and we followed, skidding and slipping and sliding along the pavement.

'I wish I could fly, I wisha, wisha, wisha, wish I could fly!' It was a good job the streets were empty because Dirk was flapping his arms as he sprinted ahead of me, his feet and legs slithering this way and that as we reached the corner.

I grabbed his arms and held him back. 'Hey, Dirk, let's walk like normal people.'

It was there.

8

The limo was parked outside the post office.

JINX 99, the number plate read.

The limo was as long as the post office and the ladies' hat shop next door put together, and shone in the ice-cold morning light like an enormous decoration on a giant's Christmas cake. 'It's brill-brill-brilliant!' Dirk was almost on his knees in worship and I was nearly there with him. It was by far the flashiest car I'd ever seen, the biggest, most eye-watering, expensive thing that had ever been driven down the streets of Hexhill-on-Sea.

'I wonder who . . . wonder who, wonder who owns it?'

There was a set of footprints in the snow from the back of the limo to the door of the post office, a set of small feet, a heel and a sole, a heel and a sole. I pointed to them and – as I told Dirk, 'That person owns it!' – out came the limo owner from the post office. She was a frail-looking old lady, wrapped up in a big brown fur coat that looked large enough to swamp her; a picture book granny with grey hair tied in a bun, round-rimmed spectacles and a face as sweet as the inside of a chocolate box. She didn't seem to notice us as she walked back to the limo, smiling, clutching her pension and peeling off the bank notes into her black leather handbag. And just as she didn't notice us, so she didn't notice a £50 note blowing out of her hand and sailing, as if in slow motion, on the ice-cold breeze right towards Dirk and me.

'Who's the driver?' I asked, speaking my thought out loud.

As the £50 note landed, face down on the snow at our feet, Dirk's mouth opened wide. I clamped my hand on his gob and hissed, 'Shut up!' As the money filled our eyes, the old lady was swallowed by the limo which went on its way down the street.

I reached down, picked up the money and looked at Dirk.

'We should've, should've called the old lady back and given her the money,' said Dirk, trying his best to get the bank note out of my hands.

'I know. I know we should have done that, Dirk, but we didn't,' I replied.

'But I wanted to. I was going to,' he told me.

'I know, Dirk, I know you were going to. That's why I covered your mouth up.'

'But it's wrong.'

'I know it's wrong, Dirk. But so's having only 4p between us. That's wrong. But now we're fifty quid better off and she's so rich she won't even notice. She didn't even notice she'd lost it.'

'I feel . . . bad about it.'

'So do I, Dirk, but to be honest, I felt even worse when we only had 4p.'

As I folded the £50 note, and quickly hid it away in my coat pocket, I noticed something quite odd about it. Although the bank note was crisp and new, the Queen's eyes were covered by a pair of dark blue ink blots. I turned it over to see who was on the other side. It was a man called Sir Christopher Wren (1632–1723), and there was a bubble drawn coming out of his mouth, with the words: *My name is Wren but I cannot fly* . . . written inside.

'That's strange!' said Dirk.

'Who cares?' I replied. 'It's money. And it looks like one of your wishes is about to come true, Dirk.'

TUESDAY 3rd FEBRUARY

Chapter 3

Overnight there was a massive thaw and at half past eight in the morning a personal message came over the radio from Mr Spanner himself. 'Parents, boys and girls of Hexhill County Primary School, just to let you know: Today, school is open! No excuses for not turning in and don't be late! The buses are running normally and the roads are clear so . . . get to school right now!'

It was a long, long day and time moved like a snail with a stone shell on its buckled back. When we got back into class after last play, Miss Harper, our teacher, looked twice as fed up as we felt.

OUR DAY OFF SCHOOL

She'd chalked the words on the board while we'd been on the yard and as we sat down, she called, 'I want at least a whole page. No talking, no getting out of your seats, no daydreaming, just write, write, write!'

So I wrote a whole page, filled the blank sheet as fast as I could, so that I could stop writing and stare out of the window.

There was a smell of damp in the room and the wind was leaking in through the gaps at the edges of the windows. I saw Isis heading quickly for the warmth of the caretaker's shed for a saucer of milk and a sleep. Lucky old Isis, I thought, as I felt Miss Harper's eyes on the back of my head and her breath on my neck.

'Ellie, you're daydreaming!' she whispered.

'Sorry, Miss. I'm thinking what to write next, Miss,' I lied.

She picked up the sheet and squinted at it, clearly dismayed at the poor state of my handwriting.

'Well then, Eleanor Beckett, perhaps you'd like to read what you've written for us.'

When I took my time, my writing looked a mess but when I rushed it looked like the work of a cack-handed alien. 'Come on, Ellie,' said Miss. 'Get on with it.' Miss Harper was lots of thing but patient wasn't one of them. Across the classroom, Shane Sharples, our next door neighbour and deadliest enemy, was grinning into his hand, enjoying the sight of me being put on the spot by Miss.

My account of the day off wasn't exactly a hundred per cent honest. I hadn't written about that part of the day when we got home and had to stash the sleigh in a neighbour's hedge and how we had to get it out later when Mum and Dad went to the pub and how we had to hide it in the garage because we didn't have an answer to the question they'd have surely asked, '*Where did you get the money for that then*?'

I cleared my throat, got to my feet, and read out loud, 'Our Day Off School'.

'We'd been saving up for ages, me and my twin brother Dirk that is, for ages and ages, doing paper rounds and washing cars and that, doing odd jobs for people and neighbours and keeping the money in the post office for a long time. We saved up about fifty quid. When we woke

16

up and saw it'd been snowing, Dirk said, "Let's buy a sleigh!" I said, "OK!" So we went to Doran's Department Store and got one and went sleighing on it down the sand dunes on the beach and at first it was rubbish because the snow was too powdery but as soon as the snow packed down hard into thick ice it was brilliant, better than a fairground ride. Dirk thought it was like flying, to me it was just sleighing but it felt brilliant anyway. It took my breath away and turned my guts over. It made my eyes sting and ears buzz. The wind felt like a giant snowman burping into my face. Dirk said he kind of felt the same. So we stayed on the dunes for hours and hours and hours and only went home when the stars and moon started taking shape in the sky. When the sky went dark, when outer space came to life.'

I thought Miss Harper was going to kiss me. She clapped her hands on my shoulders and said, 'Ellie, that's so . . . it's like . . . poetry!'

'It is?' She took the book from my hands and frowned at the writing.

'The handwriting's a bit grim,' she went on, 'but we can work on that! This is the best you've ever done, the best work I've seen for years.'

'It is?'

I could feel the whole class looking at me, my face burning up and was as glad as I'd ever been to hear the bell ringing for the end of the day. As we lined up at the door, I could see the smirk on Shane Sharples' ratty face had turned into a jealous frown and that I loved to see. Miss dropped my book into her big black bag and smiled at me, saying, 'You'll have to write this up on the computer, Ellie.'

'What? All of it, Miss?'

'You can do it during Maths, you can have the computer to yourself, Ellie!'

Together, as we filed out of class, Dirk and I turned and Shane looked like he'd just swallowed a lump of rotten fish. It was even better than the Christmas morning when Shane'd been posing on his brand new £400 mountain bike and crashed it into the side of his dad's BMW.

Chapter 4

Talking of expensive cars, when we got home from
school there was a Range Rover outside the house, one
I'd never seen before, and I was suddenly filled with a
mighty sense of doom. Dempsey, our brown brindle
Boxer dog, was on the bottom stair, looking totally
miserable and peering into nowhere.

'Ellie! Dirk!' Mum erupted into the hallway and waved
at us to join her in the living room which looked like
someone'd swept out our attic and dumped the lot on the
carpet and furniture. Dad was on the sofa between a pair
of visitors, a man and a woman.

Oh no! I thought. *It's the police!* They've found out
about the £50 note and have come with a warrant to
search the place. My thoughts raced straight to the garage
and I wondered if they'd been in there yet and why they
were looking at the family photo albums. The visitors
looked at me and Dirk and smiled this plastic sort of
smile.

'This is Sally and this is Dave,' said Mum. 'They're
from BBC Television!'

'We're from "Where Are They Now?"' Dave told me.

'We're going to make a film about your mum and dad,'
Sally dictated. 'Won't that be something?'

I was glad it wasn't to do with the £50 note, I was glad
it wasn't the police, but this wasn't good news. ' "Where

Are They Now?"' I said. 'The programme which digs up people who used to be famous and shows the country what they're like years later now that they're not famous anymore, so that everyone can laugh at them...!' It was dawning on me what was about to happen and I felt like being violently sick, there and then, on the carpet.

'I wouldn't put it like that,' said Sally, still smiling but not with her eyes.

'I don't want anything to do with this!' I barked, walking out of the room and grabbing Dirk by the arm to take him with me. 'Dirk, time to go, bro!'

Dempsey trotted up the stairs after us while Mum stood in the hallway calling, 'Oh don't be like that, you two. Come down. This could be really good fun!'

'I'd rather swim in a barrel of slug slime than have anything to do with this!' I shouted down, before slamming my bedroom door shut, fighting back tears of shame.

Let me explain. Long ago, before they settled down in Hexhill-on-Sea as plain old Mr and Mrs Rodney and Hazel Beckett, Mum and Dad were punk rockers.

Like a lot of other middle-aged people nowadays.

Back in the old days, Dad called himself Rodney Rodent and Mum, on account of her strangely coloured beehive hairdo, went by the name of Purple Hazel.

Most people like them went through the punk rock era with nothing more to show than a set of cringeworthy photographs but not Mum and Dad. Oh no, not our moronic mum and deadbeat dad!

Mum and Dad had a hit record and there was a video to go with it. *Hey you, jump under that train!* by The Burps (the name of their band) went to number 17 in the charts, stayed around for a week or two, and, for a short time, Mum and Dad were famous.

Dirk looked at me, and asked, 'What d'you think's going to happen?'

Through the bedroom floor, the sound of *Hey you, jump under that train!* blasted into my bedroom and Dempsey slunk, whimpering, under the bed.

> *Hey you, with the plastic brain,*
> *Take a running leap, jump under that train!*
> *Gary 'n' Gerry 'n' Johnny 'n' Jayne*
> *Run off the platform, jump under that train!*

'D'you think they'll show the BBC people the video?' bawled Dirk through the horrible row from downstairs.

'Oh yes!' I said. 'Most definitely...'

On the video, Mum and Dad – each about twenty years younger and forty bags of sugar lighter between them – jumped around a completely white room, white floor, white walls, no windows, sticking their spotty faces into the camera and poking their tongues out, Dad in skin-tight leopard-skin print trousers and a torn string vest, Mum in a plastic mini skirt with a fur bikini top and a bucket of make-up on her face.

'Dirk,' I could hardly say it. 'I'm sorry to say, they'll probably show the video on TV just to remind everyone of what The Burps were like back in the old days, just so that people can sit at home and say, "Didn't they look young and stupid then, and don't they look middle aged and stupid now!"'

'This,' said Dirk, 'could be very, very, very embarrassing!'

Don't take your holidays over in Spain,
Why don't you just jump under that train!

And downstairs, so ended Mum and Dad's two-minute musical masterpiece, followed by a burst of applause and laughter from Sally and Dave from the BBC. 'We'll come over this weekend and make a film about you. The Burps then and now!' Sally was almost shouting with delight.

'The viewers will love it!' Dave told them.

Dirk looked at me. 'What are we, we, we gonna do, do, do?'

I had an idea. It was desperate and a long shot but it was the only thing I could come up with. Dirk stared at me, his eyes pleading for help. I shrugged. 'We'll try and talk some sense into them.'

'But they don't listen,' said Dirk.

'Got a better idea, Dirk?'

Chapter 5

'Mum! Dad! We've got to talk!'

They were still in the living room – Sally and Dave were long gone – they were still looking through their old photos and playing the video over and over again. I marched across the room, switched the telly off and spoke at them loudly, 'We've got to talk!'

'Don't tell me,' said Dad. 'You've changed your minds and you want to be a part of the programme, you want to be a Burp!'

'No!' said Dirk, getting in before I did. 'No way!' He turned to Mum, who'd already been at the make-up kit.

'What's the problem, kids?' she smiled.

'Mum,' I pleaded, 'the problem is,' I told her, 'they're all going to be laughing *at* you, not *with* you! Everyone who watches the programme and the people making it.'

'No, no, no!' Dad insisted. 'It won't be like that at all! Don't you see, this could be the opening of a brand new career in showbusiness for us. We'll make more records, do more shows, go on telly...'

'But that's not going to happen, Dad! They're going to put you on TV for five minutes, laugh at you and then forget all about you again!'

'What do you know?' Dad was on his feet and pointing his finger. 'Your mum and me, we were in showbusiness over twenty years ago, we were even on "Top of the

Pops".'

I looked at Mum but she just laughed and said, 'What've we got to lose?'

'Your dignity,' I replied.

They shared the strangest glint in their eyes. I could have talked to them until my teeth turned blue but Mum and Dad just weren't going to listen.

I stopped at the door and said, 'There's one thing I'd like to know. Who contacted the BBC? Was it you, Dad? Or was it you, Mum?'

They looked at each other, totally blankly, shrugged, shook their heads.

'Someone in the neighbourhood put them onto us,' Dad grinned.

'That's right,' Mum agreed. 'Sally phoned up this morning and asked if they could come over.'

WEDNESDAY 4th FEBRUARY

Chapter 6

Assembly happened every morning at ten o'clock, in the hall where we also did PE and Games, where we also ate our dinners and where it always smelled of stale food, floor polish and sweaty feet.

I wound up near the front of the line, cross-legged on the floor behind Dirk, mouthing the words of *Think of a World without any Colours*, without really singing, as Spanner marched up and down in front of the wall bars, barking death threats at the kids who were caught not joining in.

'Dirk,' I whispered, 'Spanner's wearing his best blue suit!'

'And the teachers are whispering to each other!' observed Dirk. The teachers sat in a line behind Spanner, talking out of the corners of their mouths. I noticed an empty chair at the end of the row of teachers. Something was definitely going on.

As the hymn ended, Spanner flattened down his hair flap and took a deep breath. 'This morning, we've got a very special guest in school. A lady who's not only kindly volunteered to come in and help children with their reading but also . . . ' He looked at the swing doors. 'A lady who's come in to donate a large cheque to the school fund.' The doors opened smoothly, as if pulled open by a pair of invisible hands and as she walked in a splinter of

27

fear pierced my spine. 'Boys and girls!' said Spanner. It was *her*. 'Say good morning to Mrs Nijinsky!' It was *her*, the old lady from the limo who dropped the £50 note.

'Good-mor-nin'-Miss-is-Ni-jin-sky!' Three hundred children spoke in one sing-song voice.

Dirk turned to face me, his mouth wide with amazement, his eyes dizzy with disbelief. 'But it, but it, but it can't be *her*!' he said.

'Oh, but it is!' I told him as I looked through the plate glass on the far end of the hall and there, in between the teachers' beaten-up Escorts and battered-out Robin Reliants, the white limo stood out like a unicorn in a field of donkeys.

'Turn around, Dirk!' I hissed. She was a metre away from us. She was smiling as her eyes scanned the faces in the hall. Her eyes were zig-zagging towards the front, her eyes settled on the front rows and picked me out. I forced myself to keep my eyes on her, not to blink, to meet her gaze, but as she spoke, she seemed to speak straight to me. 'Good morning!'

I looked away and suddenly felt how the £50 note had been in my hand, damp and slightly rough, as I handed it to the assistant in Doran's and Dirk picked up the sleigh.

'Mrs Nijinsky,' Spanner informed us, 'has kindly offered to present our school with a very large cheque.'

Mrs Miles, the deputy head, stepped forward, smiling a false smile, pointing the school camera at Mr Spanner and Mrs Nijinsky. As Mrs Miles snap snap snapped away, Mrs Nijinsky seemed to produce the cheque from thin air. Spanner stopped squeezing his hands together and reached out to grab it from her but Mrs Nijinsky stepped back and told him, 'I'd like to present the cheque to a child.' She had the kindest, sweetest voice.

'Oh, most certainly!' Spanner was oozing, sliming and smiling at her.

She pointed at our row, her finger picking out Dirk. 'Young man, would you care to stand up?' Dirk didn't react at all so I poked him between the shoulders and told him, 'Get up, get the cheque and give it to Spanner!'

Mrs Nijinsky's hands settled on Dirk's shoulders as he showed the cheque to the whole school. A gasp of real amazement echoed around the hall, as Spanner read the tiny writing, '*Pay Hexhill County Primary School the sum of...one thousand pounds, £1000.* Why, thank you, Mrs Nijinsky!' Spanner snatched the cheque from Dirk's hands and with that a round of applause rang about the place followed by a buzz of conversation.

'Spend it wisely, Mr Spanner!' She spoke to the Head Teacher but her eyes were fixed, smiling straight into mine as she folded a hand on Dirk's head.

Dirk turned his face to look at her. 'You must be worth a bomb, lady!'

The teachers laughed but I could tell that Dirk's remark embarrassed them. Mrs Nijinsky had her hands clamped around Dirk's face so he couldn't look away from her and she was looking at him like a long-lost grandson. She whispered something in his ear and Dirk just smiled and nodded back at her before coming back to his space at the front of the line. My heart was doing little somersaults and my brain spun in my skull.

'What'd she say, Dirk? What'd she say?' Spanner stomped his foot and bellowed for silence.

A hush fell on the hall as Mrs Nijinsky settled down on the empty seat at the end of the line of teachers and Dirk replied, 'I'll tell you later, Ell!'

Chapter 7

But ten minutes later, Dirk had forgotten. When we got out of the hall and I asked him again what Mrs Nijinsky had said, Dirk just couldn't remember.

'It's gone, Ellie! Sorry...'

All morning I was tortured by not knowing. I couldn't follow a single thing Miss Harper said because my brain was burning from the inside out, my scalp was crawling with curiosity: What the hell did old Jinxy say to Dirk on the quiet? Every chance I had, I cornered Dirk.

'Did she mention money?' I asked.

'What money?'

'Any money... like fifty quid?'

'No.'

'Thank God for that. Think, Dirk, think, lad!'

'I can't remember...'

It wasn't warm in school but all morning I sweated buckets. When we sat down to eat our packed lunch in the hall, I'd just about given up hope of finding out what she'd whispered to him when Dirk gazed over at the spot where she'd handed him the big cheque and announced, 'Now, I remember...'

'Quick,' I blurted, 'before you forget, what was it she said?'

'She said, you're welcome to come to my house anytime you like! Bring your sister if you like. And some other stuff.'

'How did she know you had a sister?'

'She said, bring your sister if you've got a sister,' Dirk replied.

'So where does she live, old Jinxy!'

'Don't be calling her names, she's Mrs Nijinsky!'

'Where does Mrs Nijinsky live?'

'Hexhill Lighthouse . . . '

And I didn't pay the slightest bit of attention to lessons that afternoon. Hexhill Lighthouse loomed tall in my mind. Because the thing about Hexhill Lighthouse was that no one had lived there for years, it was an old wreck and everyone in town who boasted they'd ever been near the place had to admit it sent shivers round your skull and chills down the back of your neck. The Jinx herself had told Dirk that she'd grown up there all those years ago, the daughter of the last Lighthouse Keeper in Hexhill. She was doing the place up, making it into a nice home so that she could spend her days in the height of comfort with a view of the sea and an ocean of memories.

'I wonder if she meant it was OK to call round tonight?' I asked Dirk.

'She said to call anytime,' he said. 'And tonight's anytime, I guess.'

Chapter 8

By the time we arrived home, Burp mania had taken over the house. When we opened the front door, they were in the hallway – Mum and Dad in all their punk glory.

'I see you've been to the hairdresser's,' Dirk observed, pointing at Dad's head which was now shaved, save for a green mohican strip that ran across the centre of his skull, pulled up into seven sharp points. Mum gave us a twirl in her thigh length boots and the yellow hospital binbag that she wore as a dress.

'What do you think?' she said, patting the walls of her newly re-built purple beehive hairdo.

'I think you look like a pair of middle-aged bubble heads!' I snapped. Dad sneered at me and strummed the strings of the electric guitar that was hanging from his neck. I grabbed Dempsey's lead from behind the front door and clipped it to his collar as Mum tapped the microphone in her hand and said, 'Testing, testing...' There was a huge amplifier behind them that rose up to the ceiling that echoed and whined.

'We've got one thing to say to you, one thing, and one thing alone!' He turned the volume switch up high and Mum's voice bellowed through the speakers, 'Dirk! Ellie! Dempsey!' She pointed at each of us in turn. 'Hey you, jump under that train!'

We ran out of the house, Dirk, Dempsey and me; we ran down the street as fast as we could with the live sound of Mum and Dad's one hit record chasing after us through the thickening darkness.

We walked along the cliff path, overlooking the sea on one side and the edge of town on the other with night falling down like a curtain of thick black gas. Below us, the sea heaved and sighed against the rocks, lullabies for the ghosts of sailors lost at sea.

I kept a tight hold on Dempsey's lead and steered Dirk by the arm from the edge of the cliff. 'Look where you're going, soft lad!' I warned him. A handful of stone broke from the edge and clattered to the darkness down below but, strangely, Dirk didn't seem to notice how he'd flirted with a fall; his eyes were dreamy and had a faraway look.

'What are you thinking?' I asked him but he didn't reply at first, just pointed to the sky where the full moon came out from behind a band of passing cloud.

'It makes me feel funny!' he said. I, too, felt funny. Up ahead, along a narrow winding path, Hexhill Lighthouse loomed like a giant frozen by moonlight.

A late-to-bed seagull flapped out of nowhere and right over our heads and Dirk let out a small gasp of fear. 'All right are you, Dirk?'

'I am, I am, I am, all-all-all right-right!'

There was a huge wrought-iron fence all around the massive garden that surrounded Hexhill Lighthouse, with a rusting pair of iron gates left open in the middle through which we could see the white limousine parked right outside the front door. At the top of the tower was a single window peering down like a great glass eye. I pointed it out to Dirk. 'That's where the light used to shine on the sea, warning the ships away from the rocks.'

The closer we came, the slower we walked and the normally fearless Dempsey was whimpering and pulling at his lead to go the other way.

'Dempsey wants to go home,' said Dirk, as the scent of wet iron from the railings filled my nose. 'I think we should do what Dempsey wants,' said Dirk. Stories I'd heard about the house, tales of headless spectres and bloodhungry vampires, people-eating plants and alien space fiends, all the beasts and body-snatching bogeymen rattled at top speed through the ghost train in my brain.

'Don't be silly, Eleanor, I'm just a nice old lady, a wealthy old woman!' I heard the Jinx speak, like she was ten centimetres behind me. I turned and there was nothing, and nobody, there. 'Did you hear anything then, Dirk?' I asked, but he looked at me blankly as we reached the gap in the main gates. 'I wonder who?' I thought aloud, looking at the limousine. 'If Jinxy's riding in the back seat, who's driving up front?'

Dempsey rooted his bottom to the ground, his legs, head and spine shaking with fear as moonlight bounced from the windows and the night wind sailed by, like it was moved by some invisible hand. I crouched down and placed an arm around the dog to soothe him down but he just made this weird little frightened noise in the back of his throat, a bit like the one I felt like making but couldn't, in case I freaked out Dirk who was looking very pale by now.

I checked my digital wristwatch and told Dirk, 'Listen, big brother, it's 6:03, and Mrs Nijinsky's probably eating her supper. Let's leave her in peace and come back on Saturday, when it's daytime.'

As we ran back – along the way we'd walked – down the clifftop path, I scoured the thousands of lights of the town down below, trying to single out the nuthouse we called home and wishing we were already there.

THURSDAY 5th FEBRUARY

Chapter 9

I caught Shane Sharples looking at me, with one jealous eye and one eye loaded with hate; he was jealous of me because Miss had put me on the computer to type up my work 'Our Day Off School'. And – for one thing at least – he hated me because of a little incident that took place just before Christmas. Shane looked down the end of his massive nose as Dirk wandered out of the room to go for his extra reading lesson so I bunched a fist to warn him, to remind him of what went down during the season of peace and goodwill to all men. The grin soon left his stupid face.

Shane was the reason why I was kept in by Mr Spanner for the last two weeks of the Christmas term. You see, I tried to knock Shane out and would have managed it, had it not been for Dirk pulling me off the little toerag, though, strangely enough, Dirk was the reason why I battered Shane in the boys' toilets in the first place. When it was time to face the music in Spanner's office, I wasn't sure what upset our Head Teacher the most. The fact that I'd nearly murdered Shane or that I'd gone into the boys' toilets to do it.

Back in September, Miss Harper gave us all an individual reading test to see where we were up to and because Dirk only came out with a 6.2-year-old reading age, he was withdrawn from class on Thursday mornings to get extra help. Shane, who was given the job of tidying Miss' desk, read the reading scores and wasted no time in making up a football chant which caught on around the school like measles in a children's home.

Six point two, six point two
Dirk's got a brain like a ball of poo!

When I caught up with Shane, outside the boys' loo, he told me, 'Yeah I did make it up. So what!' His last words to me as he disappeared inside were, 'And what are you going to do about it, *Eleanor*?' His next words, as I swung him round by the hair, were, 'Get off me, please, I'm begging you, Ellie! I'm begging you!'

Mum and Dad were called in and given a bill for the cracked sink, and the broken cubicle door, and the damage to the water pipe, and the hinge on the main door.

And I was about as popular as an ice-cream van at the North Pole. Even though Shane started the trouble with his stupid song skitting Dirk, nobody in school, except for Miss Harper (who seemed to cool off from Sharples after this), listened to me.

But, then again, the good thing was all of a sudden, nobody in school seemed to remember the words to the song. Or if they did remember they didn't seem to want to sing it anymore.

Chapter 10

It was nearly lunch time and Dirk had been out of class for much longer than he usually was for his extra reading lesson. I was on my way back from the staffroom, where I'd been to put Miss Harper's potato in the microwave, when I heard Dirk's voice, and his laughter, echoing out of the empty classroom at the end of the corridor. He was reading out loud, quite quickly, and much more clearly than usual, *'The boy tied the wings to his arms and...'* He turned the page over. *'...watched the birds to see how they used their wings to fly...'* I hadn't heard Dirk read as well as this, ever. There wasn't one pause, not one tripping up over an awkward word, not one hint of a hiccup.

I reached the classroom door and peeped round the corner into the room. Mrs Nijinsky was sitting next to Dirk and pointing to the words in the book as he read along. I said nothing, stayed as quiet as I could in the doorway until I had a sudden coughing fit and they both looked at me, at once.

'Ellie!' Dirk sounded surprised to see me, as if he'd just landed feet first in the real world from the make believe of his story book.

'Eleanor!' said Mrs Nijinsky. 'I've heard so much about you. Come in, dear.' Eleanor? Strangely, the sound of my whole name made goosebumps pitter patter up and down my spine. But she had a lovely smile, a smile that made you want to walk right over and sit at her feet, and stare up into her bright blue little old lady's eyes. I felt myself smiling back, staring into her eyes when suddenly the £50 note floated by my mind's eye and I felt the smile slip quickly from my face.

'Is something wrong, Eleanor?' asked Mrs Nijinsky. 'You look a little pale.'

Something most definitely was wrong. I felt very guilty for taking the money, and I was gripped by a fear that I couldn't begin to explain, the same fear I used to feel when I was five years old and I woke up in the night, in the darkness.

'I'm...I'm all right, Mrs Jinx...' She laughed, and Dirk laughed too, before I had the chance to correct my slip of the lip.

'Mrs Nijinsky, Ni-jin-sky,' the old lady chuckled.

'I'm sorry, Mrs Nijinsky.' The number plate on the limo, JINX 99, flashed before my eyes as it headed down the snowbound street and I wafted the £50 note under Dirk's nose. 'Sorry, Mrs Nijinsky,' I said, feeling myself turn scarlet and wishing I could shrink to the size of a pea and slip down a crack between the floorboards.

'Whatever for?' she asked. 'Whatever for?'

'For getting your name wrong!' I replied.

The lunch time bell rang and school was filled with the sound of scraping chairs, slamming desks and the footsteps of hundreds of hungry children. She handed the reading book to Dirk and smiled. 'You can keep the book, Dirk, because you read very, very well indeed.' She ran a hand across Dirk's head and he glowed in her attention, reminding me of a cat being stroked by its owner. 'Time for lunch, Dirk,' she told him, as he walked to the door, backwards, watching her, smiling at her.

Chapter 11

Dirk shouted on top decibel to beat the bone-shaking noise of the dining room but, as we ate our Dairylea and peanut butter sandwiches, I had to strain to hear what he was saying. He hadn't shut up about her since she'd sent him on his merry way half an hour earlier. I threw the crust of my last buttie into the box and gave up trying to listen and eat at the same time.

'It's like she...' As a dinner plate clattered to the floor, a surge of noise, cheering and laughing, drowned Dirk out.

'Dirk, I can't hear you, mate!'

'I said, it's like she makes the words real easy to read, just by sitting there and pointing at them. They usually look like a pan of alphabetti-spaghetti but when Mrs Nijinsky's there, it's like... it's like...'

'Magic!' I shouted.

'Yeah, just like magic,' Dirk replied. 'She's so, so, so nice to me. I used to hate reading books.' He pulled out the reading book she'd given him and looked at it with love in his eyes. 'It's such a good story.'

I reached across and said, 'Well, let's have a look!'

It was called *Greek Myths and Legends* and had a picture on the cover of a boy and a man with strapped-on wings, flying off an island across a deep blue sea.

'What's the story you're reading to her?' I asked,

thinking that it was one thing to be able to read the words all of a sudden but wondering if Dirk had got the point of what he was reading. He pointed at the cover and came over all grown up and intelligent.

'It's about this lad called Icarus and his dad and they're trapped on this island by this King, and they're kept prisoner on the island and they want to escape and the only way they can do this is by flying off the island and because they're only people they can't do this so the dad watched the birds and sees the way they fly and they start collecting feathers and making big wings of their own that they can strap onto their arms and fly away...'

He stopped to draw breath.

'And?' I asked.

'And,' said Dirk. 'That's about as far as we got.'

'That's great, Dirk, I'm really pleased. You can read the rest to me later.'

'I'd rather read round at Mrs Nijinsky's lighthouse on Saturday.'

'Say that again, Dirk.'

'On Saturday, she's asked us over for the day.' The noise around us suddenly seemed to fade away. 'She said we could go round and I could read to her. I asked her: Is the lighthouse as spooky on the inside as it is outside?'

'What did she say?'

'She said it's a nice house, that it only looks spooky at night, that there's nothing to be afraid of. She said we could do a few odd jobs and she'd pay us for helping out.'

45

'How can she live in it?' I asked. 'It's a . . . it's an old dump!'

'She's not living in all of it yet, just a few rooms till it's been done up and decorated,' Dirk told me as he eyed my chocolate biscuit.

'Help yourself!' I told him, my usually huge appetite gone. 'Listen, Dirk, did she mention losing the fifty quid?' His mouth was full, so he just shook his head.

'Good,' I said. 'That's good!' But feeling good I wasn't.

Chapter 12

That night, I woke up from a very bad dream. Dirk and me were dressed in black and standing at Mrs Nijinsky's grave while the undertakers lowered the coffin into the ground. Dirk was crying but this man – I didn't see his face – said, 'Don't cry, Dirk! She's left all her money to you, everything, the house, the limo, the lot.'

So, Dirk stopped crying and suddenly a pair of huge stuck-on wings, like the ones in the Greek storybook, appeared on him and he was flying and I called for him to come down but he wouldn't listen and he just went higher and higher and I knew he was in terrible danger and... the wings dropped off and he started hurtling down to earth, and he was screaming as he tumbled into the open mouth of Mrs Nijinsky's grave... and I woke up.

I jumped out of bed and hurried to his room to see if he was all right, and found him standing at the window.

'Say, Dirk, are you OK?'

'Come here, Ellie.' He pointed out of the window. 'Look, you can see Hexhill Lighthouse from here. I'd never noticed before.'

The lighthouse loomed up from the cliffs like a one-eyed giant guarding the coast beneath a star-speckled sky. Dirk handed me his binoculars and said, 'I think there's something on the roof.'

A pair of tiny green lights flashed on and off, caught in the moonlight, as something moved across the slates of the domed roof and along the cracked guttering.

'I think it's. . . it's a cat,' I observed.

'A cat?' Dirk sounded surprised. 'But she hates animals . . . ' He walked away from the window, climbed into bed and whispered, 'Goodnight, Ellie.'

'What do you mean, *she hates animals*?'

'Goodnight, Ellie!' He turned his back to me and pulled the covers over his head.

'Night, Dirk,' I wished him, leaving the room. 'I'll see you in the morning.'

But I went right back in there, feeling troubled by what Dirk had told me.

'Dirk, what do you mean Mrs Nijinsky hates animals?' But I could tell by his breathing and the light snoring, Dirk was already asleep. Or if he was pretending, he was making a frighteningly good job of it.

FRIDAY 6th FEBRUARY

Chapter 13

There was a crowd of mums, dads and children gathered at the entrance of the school, a crowd through which we weaved and shoved to get to the front to see what the fuss was over. It was a notice pinned to the door.

REWARD £50
CAT MISSING

GOOD MONEY PAID FOR INFORMATION
LEADING TO RETURN OF CAT
ANSWERS TO ISIS!
PEDIGREE SIAMESE
SEE MR SLATER (CARETAKER).

Beneath the notice was a photocopied picture of Mr Slater holding the missing cat in his arms and, looking at the photo, I suddenly felt very sorry for him. It hit me that he had no family and, when it came to friends, Isis was just about all he had. I read the notice out loud for Dirk's benefit and turned to offer a word of comfort to him but, to my surprise, he looked totally unbothered by the news.

'It's probably only gone for a walk,' said Dirk. 'Looking for some sucker to feed and pamper it for a few days before making its way back to school to old man Slater.' I followed Dirk as he elbowed his way out of the crowd. 'And anyway,' he went on, 'if the thing isn't back in the next few days, at least he can stop wondering what's happened to it. It'll have been run over or starved to death in some garden shed. Stupid Isis! Stupid cat!'

I was shocked. It was Dirk saying these things, Dirk, my softhearted, woolly-headed, animal-loving cream cake of a twin brother, who I thought I knew like the ends of my fingers and the tips of my toes.

'But, Dirk,' I said, speaking to the back of his head, as he strutted away. 'I thought you liked cats, Dirk?'

'No, not really!' He glanced at me. 'Especially not Isis. Like you said, Ellie, she's sly, she's got nine lives anyway, more than you and me, she'll probably see us in our graves.'

'Yeah, I know I said those things, Dirk ... but you don't want to listen to *everything* I say. Sometimes, I just ... I just say things. Hey, Dirk, is all this because she scratched you the other day? Dirk? Dirk!'

He was running and I had the cold sensation I'd been talking to myself. He was heading round the side of the school building, and I chased after him.

'If she's not trapped in a garden shed, she'll be in a tin of dog food, chunky choice cat meat.' Dirk laughed his head off and legged it like an Olympic athlete down the back of the school and collapsed onto the grass verge. 'She could even be in a burger now, a cat burger in a sesame bun ...'

'Hey, Dirk, cut it out, OK! Don't say things like that!'

'Why?' he asked, making it to his full height, and looming over me.

'Because old man Slater's coming and he might hear you.'

The arrival of Slater seemed to calm Dirk down. The caretaker looked like someone had sucked the life out of him. His eyes searched the distances around us, looking out, I guessed, for Isis. Normally, he'd have shouted and chased us from this out-of-bounds spot, but not this morning.

'Seen any sign of Isis, Eleanor?' He was one of the few people who gave me my full name.

'I'm afraid not, Mr Slater.'

'Well, if you do see her...?'

'I'll tell you straight away. When did she go missing?'

'Some time on Wednesday. Last time I saw her, Wednesday morning,' he said.

'When the Jinx was here!' I muttered the thought aloud. I don't know where it came from or how it happened into my head, but in the twinkling of an eye, there it was and out of my mouth.

But Mr Slater either didn't hear me or didn't reply, but just kept moving on.

'What was that?' asked Dirk.

'Oh nothing,' I replied. 'Just thinking out loud.'

'Something about Mrs Nijinsky?'

'Oh no, Dirk, I said *links*. Isis might be on the golf links.'

The bell rang and as we ran back to school, I saw Shane Sharples making his way through the gates, looking over at us, and grinning the way he did when he thought I couldn't see his face properly.

Chapter 14

Miss Harper told the class that when we got back from dinner there'd be a nice surprise waiting for us. When she spoke to us, she kept glancing around our faces, catching my eye time and time again which made me wonder whether she was going to give us the OK to beat up Shane Sharples to a pulp with me having first go.

But it wasn't that. It was to do with the massive display board that stretched right across the back wall of the classroom.

When we got back from dinnerime, Miss Harper had clearly been very busy stripping the old Tudor Kings and Queens display down and replacing it with a brand new one of creative writing by the class.

At the heart of the display, she'd stuck up a cut-out silhouette of a big sledge with my computer-typed version of 'Our Day Off School' beautifully mounted in the middle of the sledge, framed by cotton wool snowflakes.

'You've all done work to be proud of,' she told us, as we sat around her feet on the mat during afternoon register, 'but I was most impressed by Ellie's account of her day off on Monday and what she got up to with Dirk!'

Shane was grinning at his friend Warren 'Wart Boy' Bell who started laughing behind his hand. 'Warren,' said Miss, totally missing Shane, who now sat like an angel.

'Warren Bell, if you want to laugh, go and laugh outside!' Wart Boy frowned and started to pick at his knuckles where a fresh crop of seedy warts was mushrooming.

Miss Harper produced my original draft from beneath the register on her lap and started to read, '"Our Day Off School" by Ellie Beckett.' As her mouth opened and my lies flowed out, *We'd been saving up for ages, me and my twin Dirk that is ... doing paper rounds ...* my stomach turned and churned like a storm out at sea and in my mind I was back outside the post office, watching the Jinx get back into the limo and picking the £50 note up. *'We saved up about fifty quid.'* I imagined the car stopping and Jinxy getting out and saying, 'That's a form of stealing and you know it!'

The pulse in my wrist was ticking like a bomb and my palms were leaking into each other as Miss read on, *'... when the stars and moon started taking shape in the sky. When the sky went dark, when outer space came to life.'*

Miss pointed to the display board. 'Would anyone like to ask Ellie a question?' she asked, and I felt like a victim must've done in a medieval torture chamber when the thumbscrews were jangled under her nose. Leila Ross, a girl with hair like candy floss, asked, 'Ellie, that's dead poetic. Do you like poetry writing?'

'Yeah, I like that.' I couldn't meet her eyes, my face was flaring.

Sam Trent, who looked like a gink but talked like a genius, said, 'You write really well about real life. Would you like to be a journalist one day?'

'No thanks,' I snapped.

But Sam pressed on, 'Dirk, do you remember the day the same way that Ellie did, or was your version of events different?'

'Good question, Sam,' Miss chimed in. 'Did it happen like Ellie wrote it, Dirk?'

There was a long silence, during which Dirk's face twisted and creased, his lips puckered and parted, as he thought about the question.

'No, not exactly, it isn't all how I remember it. No, not quite.'

I felt like I was about to fall from a very great height into a hole which didn't ever quite end.

'It was a bit different to the way Ellie wrote it.'

I looked at Dirk, but he wasn't looking back. (*Shut up, Dirk! Shut up, Dirk!* I thought, urging the words into his mind) but he was looking at Miss who was waiting for him to spill the gravy.

'Ellie said the wind felt like a giant snowman burping into her face. But I didn't feel like that. The wind felt like a giant's hand picking me up, blowing my back, making me fly even if I didn't want to anymore. But I do want to fly. I wish I could fly like the boy in the story. That's all really.'

For a horrible moment, I thought Dirk was going to cough up the truth about the fifty quid. The relief when he didn't bang us in the doodah was brilliant.

'Good, Dirk, good. Any more questions for Ellie ... or Dirk?' asked Miss Harper.

Shane raised his hand. 'Yes, Miss. I'd like to ask Ellie

a question, Miss.' He had a vile grin on his face, his piggy eyes twinkling with delight. 'Ellie, is there anything nice going on in your house this weekend? Anything you want to tell the class about?'

How did he know? How did he know about the BBC? And Mum and Dad? And 'Where Are They Now?'

'No!' I snapped, giving him an evil look that did nothing to straighten out his crooked grin.

'But, aren't the BBC coming round to do a film about your mum and dad because they used to be punk rockers?'

'The BBC?' Miss Harper sat up a little on her chair.

'Oh yes, Miss,' Shane gloated. ' "Where Are They Now?" Isn't that right, Ellie? They're making a film about Mr and Mrs Beckett. Rodney Rodent and Purple Hazel used to be in a band called The Burps!' The class collapsed around me into helpless fits of giggling and snorting and howling as Shane brought out an old poster. Even Miss Harper was smiling and trying not to laugh.

'How did you know? How, Shane?'

'They want to film from our garden and had to ask permission. They want to film your mum and dad from our garden, sort of showing what it's like to live next door to a family of weirdos.'

I wanted to kill him there and then, pick him up by the throat and hurl him through the window. It was him, he was the one who'd told the BBC. *Someone in the neighbourhood*, Dad had said. Someone called Shane Sharples.

It was then I had a flash of genius. Shane was enjoying my pain, so I forced myself to look like I too thought it was funny, I forced myself to smile at the poster of Mum and Dad, to chuckle a little, to point and grin, to join in with the rest of the class, to wipe the smile from Shane's face. Dirk, confused, picked up on my laughter and he too joined the class in the joke at our expense. The only one not laughing now was Shane stinking scabby scumbag Sharples. And as the joke wore thin at the edges and some of the class stopped laughing, all I did was laugh a little bit louder, pointing and grinning at Shane until Miss clapped her hands together and said, 'Right, everyone, joke over, back to our places and Geography books out!'

As he folded the poster away into his desk, he caught me looking at him and I smiled and asked, 'Was it your idea to call the BBC?'

'No!' He sounded like he was telling the truth but he was a really good liar.

'Where did you get the poster, Shane?'

'I found it in our street.'

'Liar!' I hissed.

'Cow!' he replied.

'Pig's breath!' I whispered.

'Cow! Cow! Cow!' He was getting louder and louder. 'Y'ugly little cow!' he called me in a big booming voice, as the rest of the class went dead silent. I looked at Miss, my face all hurt and surprised at Shane's outburst.

'Come here, Shane!' she shouted. 'No play for you this afternoon, you horrible specimen!'

I opened my desk lid to get my Geography and buried my head and very quietly, but with the deepest joy in my heart, laughed and laughed and laughed.

SATURDAY 7th FEBRUARY

Chapter 15

Just before seven o'clock in the morning, the people from the BBC arrived in a minibus and a car. There was a fat cameraman, an ape-like sound recordist, Sally the producer, Dave her personal assistant, a miserable-looking driver and a big bloke with some huge lights.

Just after seven o'clock, Dirk and me had Dempsey on his lead and were hitting the street with Mum chasing after us saying, 'Oh, stay and be filmed with us. It'll be a really good laugh!' She'd squeezed herself into a black rubber frock with all sorts of zips and pins, and had purple make-up on her face. Dad was in a white boiler suit with the word 'Destroy' printed all across it and a black dog collar round his throat. Goosebumps covered every piece of my skin and my teeth tingled with embarrassment.

'Well, where are you going to go all day?' asked Dad, leaning out of their bedroom window. 'Huh? They're gonna be here all day, y'know!'

'We've got somewhere to go!' I called back at him.

'The trouble with you kids is you're a pair of boring little toerags!' Mum stamped her stiletto boot, and from his bedroom window, I saw Shane looking down and laughing.

'What's this?' I blurted out, as a gang of kids from our class turned the corner, led by Wart Boy, with

Damien Dawes, Barry Flanagan and Frank Fagan at the head of the posse. 'What's this?' I asked, as they headed towards us.

Fagan pointed past us and replied, 'We're going to Shane's house. He's invited the whole class round to watch the filming. Hey, where are you two going?'

We ran to the end of the street and round the corner where more of our classmates were heading towards Shane's house.

'Just keep running,' I told Dirk. 'Don't stop to speak to anyone, just keep on your toes and let's get as far away from here as quickly as we can.'

Chapter 16

By the time we came within shouting distance of Hexhill Lighthouse, it was turning out to be a cold but very bright winter morning. We stopped on the clifftop path and caught our breath, giving me a chance to look again at the old place. I had to laugh at myself for getting my knickers in a tangle when we'd headed over on Wednesday. In the morning sunshine, with the seagulls flapping around the top of the tower, all it looked like was a ruined lighthouse. I'd been a fool to be afraid of the place and now that I had my brain working properly, I was quite eager to get inside and see how things developed between old Mrs N and the apple of her eye, Dirk.

As we passed the white limo we had a good close-up look at the bodywork and the JINX 99 number plate, while Dempsey lifted his leg against the rear wheel and had a sly slash on the tyre.

'Go on, Dirk!' I pushed him towards the door. 'You knock, it was you she invited over.' Dirk pressed the bell but it was long out of order, and then he knocked on the door. 'Louder, Dirk, or she won't hear you!' He banged with his fists and stepped back. It was a big black door with an arched top around which was a trailing ivy that was wild and thick and hung down under its own weight.

Dirk looked at me when the sound of someone fiddling with a lock on the other side came through the woodwork. The door opened and an old man peered around and out at us. He had a head crowned with a mop of grey hair, deep brown eyes and a nose as sharp as an eagle's beak. At first, he looked a little spaced out, like an old person who couldn't remember their name, but then he smiled and his face came alive with the same loving kindness as I'd seen in Mrs Nijinsky's eyes.

'Dirk . . . and Ellie?' He spoke beautifully, like an old-time actor in a black and white movie. This, I thought, must be the person who drives the limo.

'That's us. Are you Mr Nijinsky?' I asked.

He laughed, opening the door wide enough for us to head in. 'I'm afraid Mr Nijinsky died a long long time ago. Come in, don't stand out there getting cold.'

'Who is it, Charles?' Mrs Nijinsky's voice drifted past him from the hallway.

'It's Dirk and Ellie, your young friends,' he said, waving us past him into the hugest, shadow-filled hallway I'd ever been in all my life. *Her friends?* That was how she thought of us, as *her friends*. This old lady, a widow, a kind person who gave up her time to help Dirk with his reading.

Friends, I thought, some friends, friends who took her money; but even that wasn't fair to Dirk, it was me, me who really took the fifty. My gut knotted with guilt, my heart became heavy and sadness filled my head as Mrs Nijinsky appeared at the head of the wide curving staircase that split the circular hallway in two. A beam of light fell through a stained glass window and picked out the joy on her face when she clapped eyes on us. She threw her arms open and headed down the stairs, saying, 'Dirk, and Ellie too, what a delight it is to see you here. You know, I thought you weren't going to come. I thought you'd forgotten all about me.'

Dirk was walking across the hallway to meet her and when she reached the bottom of the stairs, she gave him a hug.

I'll repay the money, I thought, *I'll do jobs for her for nothing, and I'll get it back to her somehow*. I had the feeling I was being watched and turned my eyes towards Charles who was looking right at me. He smiled at me and told me, 'She's talked about nothing else all week. *Dirk and Ellie, wouldn't it be lovely if they came to visit a lonely old widow?*'

I forced myself to smile back at him though there was a very bitter taste at the back of my throat. Mrs Nijinsky led Dirk through a narrow doorway into a room at the back of the lighthouse and Charles said, 'Well, Ellie, don't stand there all day. Come and have breakfast with Mrs Nijinsky.'

Chapter 17

There was a real fire burning in the grate and as we sat close to it for warmth, with trays on our laps, Charles served up the biggest breakfast we'd ever eaten, of sugar puffs and toast, smoked bacon, scrambled egg, spicy sausages, baked beans, mushrooms, tomatoes, and cup after cup of hot, sweet, milky tea.

'More toast?' Mrs Nijinsky offered us yet another silver toastrack laden with thick diagonals of golden brown, hot buttered toast.

'I couldn't, Mrs Nijinsky,' I replied.

'I've eaten three times my usual,' Dirk told her.

'I like to see children eat a good breakfast. It means you'll be set up for the whole day ahead,' she said, as Charles gathered up the breakfast plates. I noticed she'd hardly touched her food. 'I can't eat as much myself, not at my age.' She stroked Dempsey with one hand and he fed happily from her other, all his favourite foods. Dempsey was dewy-eyed with delight and nuzzled quite fondly into Mrs N's feet and shins. 'No, I don't have the appetite I used to have,' she sighed.

'Mrs Nijinsky,' said Dirk. 'Just how old are you?'

I couldn't believe he asked that. I elbowed him but, happily, Mrs Nijinsky wasn't upset by the question. She laughed and asked, 'How old do you think, Dirk?' He shook his head. 'Have a guess?' she encouraged him, then she looked at me.

I guessed she was around seventy years old so I wiped a few years away and said, 'Sixty?' She shook her head and indicated higher with her index fingers.

'Seventy!' said Dirk.

'Higher,' she replied.

'Seventy-one,' I tried.

'Much, much higher,' she smiled.

'Er... eighty then,' Dirk guessed.

'More,' she told him. 'Much more.' We fell silent as she leaned forward and told us, 'I'm ninety-nine years old. I'll be a hundred on Friday.'

She sat back, clearly enjoying our surprise and admiration. 'Mrs Nijinsky,' I gushed. 'You don't look anything like ninety-nine. You look wonderful. You're not kidding us, are you?'

'Certainly not,' she told us. 'The reason I mention it, I was wondering if... maybe you'd like to come to my party, on Friday. It'll only be the three of us and Charles, of course, but I'd be so pleased if you could spare me some time from your young lives.'

'We'd be...' Dirk searched his head for the right words. 'Highly delighted, Mrs Nijinsky.'

As Charles took the last of the breakfast things away, he stopped in his tracks and asked us, 'Was the breakfast to your satisfaction?'

'More than to our satisfaction,' I told him. 'It was out of this world.'

'Excellent. Excellent.'

He seemed pleased with the praise as he left the room, and Mrs Nijinsky told us, 'He's a wonderful chef. He's cooked in the greatest restaurants in Europe. He's my driver, my butler, my companion, my handyman, my nurse, my secretary. He does everything for me. In fact, I don't know where I'd be without my Mr Chivers.'

Charles Chivers! I put his names together in my mind and, staring into the fire, said it over and over, quietly to myself. *Charles Chivers! Charlie Chivers!* It had a familiar ring to it and the rhythm of the words fitted in with the swing of the pendulum in the grandfather clock in the corner which suddenly chimed nine o'clock and shook me up.

'Mrs Nijinsky!' I was on my feet. 'Is there anything we can do to help you?'

'You mean a job?' she asked.

'I mean a job. We'd like to do a job for you. We don't want paying, we'd just like to do something to help you out in your new home.'

'Well,' she said, 'there's an awful lot needs doing. Lots of things need mending, old things to be thrown out, rooms that need the paper stripped from the walls and the dusty curtains pulled down.'

'Name the job, Mrs Nijinsky,' I said, the memory of a certain £50 note floating around the centre of my brain.

'There's an old ivy, a terribly untidy thing around the door. Could you cut it down for me, pull the suckers away from the bricks, get rid of the thing for me?'

'Consider it done, Mrs Nijinsky!'

Chapter 18

Charlie Chivers gave us each a pair of gardening gloves to protect our hands and a warning about the ivy. 'Be careful, Dirk and Ellie. It's quite, quite poisonous, you know.'

It took us the whole day and we stuffed over forty black bin bags with wild straggling ivy. The more we dragged down from the walls, the more seemed to appear from behind it, as if the ivy was growing out of the lighthouse. But as the first wisps of dusk appeared above the tower, Dirk looked down from the top of the ladder and said, 'I think we've got rid of it now, Ellie.'

'Ellie!' I heard my name again, a split second later like an echo, and Charles Chivers was standing behind me with two mugs of hot drinking chocolate. 'You've done a good job, you really have. Here,' he said, handing me a drink. 'Enjoy!' And enjoy it I did. I was amazed at the passage of time. Eight hours had been and gone in the space of what felt like eight minutes.

'Ellie, take the ladders back to the shed when you've finished.' He'd been out to us all day with hot drinks like this and soup to keep us going. The chocolate drink warmed me through against the cold that gripped each and every bone in my body but as I looked around to thank him, Charlie was gone.

We carried the ladders around to the back of the lighthouse where there was a garden that looked like it was trying to look like a rain forest, that was as big as an average-sized park. The back garden was hemmed in by a sandstone wall that stretched to the very edge of the clifftop. I had the strangest feeling that I was poised on the edge of the world.

We were heading for the broken-down toolshed, somewhere near the bottom of the garden, when we were stopped in our tracks at a sound of crying.

'Did you hear that?' Dirk asked. 'Sounds like a cat to me.' The crying continued, louder this time, from off the side of the narrow path.

'It is a cat,' I said, thinking how much it sounded like a hungry baby. The noise was coming from a large concrete box, like a square stone room that had been plonked in the garden and overgrown with shrubs and weeds. I laid my end of the ladder down and told Dirk, 'Keep a lookout!'

'What, what, isa-isa-is it?'

'It's an old air raid shelter.' The entrance wasn't only blocked by the head-high grass and weeds but by old doors propped against it, and it was from in here that the crying grew louder.

'Sounds like Isis,' said Dirk who suddenly ran over, calling, '£50 reward!'

'It's coming from in there!' I said, pointing at the shelter. 'You'd need a bomb to get in.'

'Excuse me!'

I heard the sound of his voice and felt it like a cold finger drawn down every bump on my spine. It was Charlie. I forced myself to smile at him. 'The toolshed's down there.' He picked up the front end of the ladder and handed it to me. 'Mrs Nijinsky has asked me to invite you back tomorrow to burn the ivy and start clearing the back garden. She's retired to bed for the evening but she's asked me to offer you her thanks for your hard work.'

The crying sounded again, this time over our heads as a seagull flapped by. Charlie pointed to it and said, 'Perhaps this is what took you from the path. Perhaps this was the sound you heard, the sound of the seagull.'

The sky behind his head was inky blue and his eyes were like coal but when he smiled his teeth shone like tiny white lasers.

'You will come back tomorrow, won't you?' he said. 'Mrs Nijinsky has so enjoyed having you around.'

'Yes, we'll be back,' I said. 'Tomorrow,' I said. 'First thing,' I said.

He walked away, stopping when Dirk called, 'Mr Chivers?'

'Yes, Dirk?' he turned.

'Thanks for taking care of us today,' Dirk called.

'That's what I'm here for, Dirk. To take care of you.'

Charlie Chivers smiled and I felt something sizzle, like a wet sausage in an overheated pan, at the dead centre of my brain.

SUNDAY 8th FEBRUARY

Chapter 19

Dirk was a long way off, at the bottom end the garden, building a wooden wigwam with Charlie Chivers. The idea was this: we were going to burn all the old ivy, weeds, coarse grass, thistles and rubbish that had blown into the bushes and the borders. I was digging up long armfuls of thick grass that looked like they'd been around longer than me and Dirk put together, and listening out for cat noises, when Mrs Nijinsky appeared at the back door of the house and waved me over. I threw down my fork, took a look at the air raid shelter as I went past, and made my way over.

'You've been working so hard,' she told me. 'Come inside and have a rest and a glass of lemonade.'

'Thank you,' I replied; *in the absence of Pepsi Max*, I thought.

We sat by the kitchen range with the oven door wide. Fire danced in the belly of the oven, casting light and warmth over the February chill of the musty old room. It was the middle of the morning but it felt strangely like the dead of night. As she hummed a gentle tune in the back of her throat, and the firelight thawed me out, I felt tired enough to fall fast asleep.

'Tired?' she asked.

'Mum and Dad had a party last night, they had all their

old friends round, they were playing music and dancing till four this morning. I'm worn out.'

'Why don't you have a little sleep?' My brain felt like it was made of setting cement, too heavy for my neck to hold up much longer, but deep inside me a voice whispered, *'Ellie, open your eyes and have a drink of lemo!'* I forced my eyes wide and swallowed most of the lemonade in a single, open-throated gulp. 'I'd better stay awake, Mrs Nijinsky!'

'And what were your parents celebrating?' she asked, over the rim of her glass.

'They used to be punk rock stars, for about five minutes. They think it's all going to happen again because they've been picked to go on telly. So, they had all their friends round to celebrate. It's pathetic. Middle-aged people trying to be young again, trying to fight off old age, like time never happened...' As the words splitter-splattered out, I remembered I was talking to a woman who was almost a hundred years old.

'I mean,' I said, desperately trying to think of something to say, 'I just don't understand them. What's so wrong with growing old?'

'Plenty,' she replied. *'Tempus edax rerum!'*

She was talking like a Roman soldier, so I told her, 'I'm sorry, Mrs Nijinsky, but we don't do Latin in school nowadays. What's that mean, *tempus edax rerum*?'

'It means *Time is the devourer of all things.* Don't be too hard on your parents, Ellie. One day, you may live to grow old yourself. I was your age once. In fact, when I was your age, this is where I lived, with Father.'

'Your father, he was the lighthouse keeper?'

She nodded and smiled and a faraway look crossed her face. I watched her and guessed that her mind was spiralling back down memory's time tunnel.

'When Father died, I had to move out of the lighthouse. I had no mother. I was fifteen years old at the time. I had no family to fall back on at all. I found work as a seamstress, making clothes from six in the morning till eight at night.'

'That's terrible, Mrs Nijinsky. That's just awful. How?'

'How did I end up so filthy rich sewing clothes? I didn't. I ran away from the sweatshop.' She smiled. 'I ran away to London Town, where I met and married a wealthy old man.'

'Mr Nijinsky?' I asked. She shook her head.

'Mr Nijinsky was my third husband. Mr Nijinsky was six times richer than my second husband, Mr Frost, who was three times as rich as my first husband, Mr Flynn.'

I laughed. A whirlpool of laughter swept from deep inside me and out of my throat in huge deep buckets of merriment. Mrs Nijinsky clapped her hands and joined in. 'Most men, Eleanor, are stupid. When it comes to men, it's hard to tell the wise from the stupid but it's easy to separate the rich from the poor. You want a piece of advice from a wealthy old woman? Marry a rich fool. Marry two if you can ... Three like me, maybe.'

I couldn't believe my ears. Sweetie pie old lady was a hard-headed woman with an attitude that could cut down trees. It was like being with the fairy godmother of girl power.

'What about Mr Chivers?' I asked.

'He's no fool,' she answered.

'How did you meet him?' She didn't reply. 'Mrs Nijinsky, are you OK?' She looked tired, tired and old all of a sudden. 'Mrs Nijinsky?'

She looked into the flames that skipped and licked the mouth of the oven. She sighed, then fell absolutely silent and stiller than still. My spine twitched with a sudden pang of anxiety. 'Mrs Nijinsky, are you OK?' Her eyes were open, wide open. Oh my God, I thought, she's dead.

'She sleeps with her eyes open!' Charlie Chivers stood in the doorway, looking directly at me. 'She's a lighthouse keeper's daughter, remember, ever vigilant, it's in the blood.'

How long he'd been standing there watching, or listening, I had no idea. She drew a thin draught of air through her narrowly parted lips and sighed her out breath.

'Come on,' said Chivers, beckoning me over with the smallest flick of his fingers. 'Let her rest, Eleanor.'

I stole a glance at Mrs Nijinsky. Charlie Chivers was waiting for me.

'Ready, Ellie?' he whispered. He frowned as I hesitated.

'Ready now,' I replied. He smiled as I followed.

I didn't like it. I didn't like it one bit as he glanced back at me and said, 'Excellent.'

Chapter 20

'Mr Chivers, that's the best bonfire I've ever seen in my life!' Dirk tossed another barrowload of dead weeds into the mountain of flame and I was forced to agree. Black smoke curled out of the edges as the old ivy gave in to the heat. Charlie, as I called him when he wasn't around, stood back and looked pleased with his work.

'Not a bad little blaze if I say so myself,' said Charlie. 'Just keep feeding it with all the garden rubbish and when it starts to die down a bit, there's a few old doors by the air raid shelter we can use.' As Charlie marched off back to the house, Dirk and I swapped a look.

'If we do move the doors . . . ' I said.

'There's nothing in there!' said Dirk, interrupting me.

'Pardon?'

'It was the seagull we heard last night. Isis won't be in there.' I didn't like his tone of voice. I didn't like the way he was talking to me like I was stupid or something.

'No, listen, Dirk. You were there, so was I, we both know what we heard.'

'Yeah, a sea-sea-seagull.'

'Well, I don't happen to agree with you that it was a seagull, spam head!'

'I don't agree with you. You're only a girl!' He slapped the back of my head quite hard and laughed just like Shane Sharples.

It was unfortunate for Dirk I had the wheelbarrow in my hands as he said and did this to me because I ran it straight into his legs, chopping him down at the knees and making him collapse into a writhing heap on the floor.

'Yes, I am a girl, Dirk, but I'm also ten times harder than you, so don't you forget that!' I said, as I made my way up the garden.

I stood close to the air raid shelter and listened but there was no sound. If Isis was in there she was probably too weak and exhausted to do much more than breathe. I held the edges of the door across the entrance but it was too heavy to move. Dirk was hobbling up the path with tears in his eyes, calling, 'Why'd you do that?'

'Because you said, I'm *only* a girl, and that's the sort of thing Shane Sharples says. Treat me like dirt, Dirk, and I'll do the same thing back. Now, stop feeling sorry for yourself and help me with this.'

He was limping quite badly and I wondered if I'd gone in on him a little too hard with the wheelbarrow.

'I'm sorry, Ellie!' He smiled through his pain. 'Here, let me . . . '

Dirk took one side and I took the other; together we walked the door away a little from the air raid shelter, revealing an entrance of pitch-black shadow and a smell that made you want to be sick.

'Hold the door, Dirk!'

I let go of my side and squeezed between the door and the shelter, crouching to get inside and calling, 'Pss, pss, pss, Isis!' My heart was thumping and I felt a sudden and mind-bending fear of the dark. There was no reply so I made my way further inside. And then I heard the sudden sound of the door falling back against the concrete shelter, blocking out the little daylight behind me and sending me into complete darkness.

'Dirk!' I cried, the blood racing around my brain, my breath suddenly going while he was outside, in the sunshine, laughing at me.

'Treat me like dirt, Ellie,' he said. 'And I'll do the same thing back!'

'Dirk, start pulling that door back right now!'

The place felt cold and wet and pasted with slime, slime from the bellies of slugs, with cobwebs dangling from every part of the low ceiling, cobwebs spun by fat spiders with a taste for blood. Locked inside, I could hear my heart beating behind my ribs and my scalp tingling with naked fright. I could hear Dirk's voice as he walked away. 'That'll teach you!' he laughed.

I wanted to cry and sob as I felt a cold breath smothering my hand, something furry burrowing into my fingers, and saw a pair of green eyes glinting in the darkness, like I'd seen on the roof through the binoculars on Thursday night.

'Isis? How did you get in here?' I asked and she mewed and wha-whaed at the sound of her name. 'OK, puss, I know you're scared because so am I.'

I took a deep breath. I just couldn't believe Dirk had done this, and I thought of how I was going to escape. I lay down on my back on the cold, wet earth and placed the soles of my feet against the door. I counted to three and pushed with all my strength against the wood. It moved a little but banged right back, so I shuffled down and got my feet a little higher up. I imagined I was a Chinese kick boxer and, pulling my feet way back, gave the door a massive shove. It toppled away and started to close us back in but I caught it with my feet and pushed and strained and heaved. And slowly, slowly, slowly it fell away and slammed down onto the long grass outside. Cold sunlight flooded into the shelter and over me as I lay on the ground on my back.

Isis sprang over my legs and, as soon as she hit the daylight, wandered round in a circle, confused and tired. I got up and walked out of the shelter, trying to calm the shaking in my bones. Dirk was at the bonfire, staring into the flames, unaware that I was out.

'That wasn't funny, Dirk!' I spat the words at him, but he didn't turn, move, flinch or blink. 'That was mean, stupid, and dangerous, Dirk!' I tapped him hard on the shoulder and asked, 'What got into you?'

But he just carried on staring into the flames and muttered, 'I was going to let you out.'

'I could have suffocated in there. I could have panicked and gone crazy.'

'I was getting you back, my legs are all bruised.'

I was about to say something like, *'Well, OK, we've both been out of line here, let's just forget it…'* when Charlie Chivers wandered behind us with Isis in his arms. He smiled and passed the cat into Dirk's arms.

'Take her back to the owner,' said Charlie, 'and claim the reward. £50, I believe it is.' He locked his eyes into mine. 'That's a lot of money, don't you think, Ellie?'

A cold wind swirled at my feet and a bank of angry clouds gathered in the winter sky above my head. The smile died on his face and Charlie drifted away, back towards the house.

Dirk looked at Isis and said, 'Fifty quid's worth of cat. Let's go and see Slater on the way home and claim that reward.'

Chapter 21

Mr Slater nearly screamed with happiness when he opened his front door and saw Isis asleep in Dirk's arms.

'Dirk? Eleanor? How can I ever thank you?' His eyes filled with tears as the cat woke up to the sound of his voice and hopped straight into his arms. 'Where? Where was she?' he asked.

'Trapped in an old air raid shelter.'

'Come in! Come in!' He threw his door open wide but I shook my head. 'It's getting dark. We'd better go home, Mr Slater, honestly...'

'Listen, the two of you, I haven't got the money with me but I'll get the £50 from the post office tomorrow afternoon.'

As he spoke, I turned particularly cold and then came over in a prickly heat. A deep growl of angry thunder echoed across the sky and moments later forked lightning cracked its way down into the churning sea.

'Are you all right, Eleanor?' asked Slater. 'You don't look very well.'

I didn't feel well. The idea of anyone getting £50 from the post office filled me with a sudden and horrendous sickness. Thunder exploded above us and with it, a heavy rain began to fall and I ran. I ran as fast as I could through the downpour with Dirk chasing after me, calling, 'Ellie? What's wrong? What's wrong, Ellie? Ellie? Ellie! Ellie!'

MONDAY 9th FEBRUARY

Chapter 22

When I walked through the school gates, with Dirk trailing five steps behind, a swarm of kids descended on us, all squealing questions over each other and into our faces. 'Did you have a go on the cameras?'; 'Did you see yourselves on film?'; 'When's it on the telly?' It felt like all the fresh air in the world had suddenly been sucked away leaving me choking and breathless in shrink-wrapped plastic.

For the first time in my life, I was overjoyed to hear the schoolbell ringing, calling everyone inside for morning lessons. But when we got into class, things weren't much better than they'd been on the yard.

'*My Weekend*'. Miss Harper chalked the title on the board and told the class, 'I'm sure you've all got something interesting to write about this morning,' as she looked directly at me. 'I bet you had a busy weekend, Ellie! I bet you've got loads to write about.'

'Not really, Miss. Nothing special.'

'You had special visitors, didn't you?'

I didn't reply. Shane jumped to his feet and threw his arm into the air.

'Yes, Shane?' she said, rising to the bait like a dumber than average fish.

'Miss, everyone in class called round to our street, to my house, at the weekend to see Dirk and Ellie's special visitors.'

'Everyone?' Miss sounded surprised. 'Who called round to Shane's?' she asked, and every single arm went up in the air... except for mine and Dirk's. Miss looked at me again, this time with a puzzled smile.

'We went out for the day, visiting a friend,' I explained. Shane was grinning wildly, like he was a cat's whisker away from bursting out laughing.

'Oh you should have been there, Miss! You should have seen it,' he shouted out. 'It was really funny. And it's going out on TV on Friday night. I know. I was talking to the producer.'

Conversations broke out across the classroom, sound igniting sound and, after what felt like the longest minute of my life, Miss banged on the table with a board rubber to make everyone calm down and shut up.

'All right! All right!' she snapped. 'Just get on with your work while I do the dinner register!'

I wrote the date and the title and looked around. Every single classmate started scribbling furiously with great big grins on their faces. It was clear they'd all had the best laugh of their lives at Mum and Dad and that on Friday, there was more to come with the whole country able to switch on the TV and join in the joke. I felt sick, sick and ashamed and totally angry. I stood up, swallowing back the tears and marched towards the classroom door.

'Ellie, where are you going?' asked Miss.

'Toilet, Miss, I think I'm going to be sick.'

Just then, the door of the classroom opened and Mr Spanner stepped in followed by Mr Slater, who had Isis in his arms. Everyone looked up and stopped writing. A whisper of 'Isis!', 'It's Isis!' weaved about the room.

'Dirk and Ellie Beckett!' said Mr Spanner. 'I believe congratulations and thanks are in order to you!'

'Oh yes,' I said, eyeing Shane. 'Didn't we tell you? Didn't we mention it? We rescued Isis on Sunday!'

Mr Spanner waved Dirk out from his place and the class gave us a round of applause. 'There'll be a special assembly tomorrow afternoon, in which Mr Slater will present you with your reward for bringing Isis back safe and sound.'

'Thank you, Sir!' I said, shaking Mr Spanner's hand.

'You deserve a medal, Dirk!' said Slater. 'And you, Eleanor.'

Miss Harper pressed her face close to mine and whispered, 'I thought you said you didn't do anything special at the weekend.'

'Well, Miss,' I replied. 'It was nothing really.' I threw Shane Sharples a grenade of a glance. 'I didn't want to sound like a big-mouthed moron.'

Chapter 23

The news about Dirk and me *rescuing* Isis spread around school like germs in a dirty drain and made the rest of the day a whole lot easier for both of us. Everyone seemed to forget about Mum and Dad and the BBC and by lunch time, as happens with stories spread by word of mouth, it was all blown up out of its real shape and size.

Warren Wart Boy, the nearest thing Shane had to a real friend, stopped us as we went onto the yard and said, 'I think you're both dead brave.'

'Do you?' I answered. 'Why's that?'

'Rescuing that cat from the clifftop. I heard Dirk had to hang on to your feet, Ellie, and lower you over the edge so as you could pick Isis off the little ledge where she was stranded, while the storm was lashing and the thunder was roaring and all that.'

'That's right,' said Dirk, coming over all serious. 'Look at this, Warren!' He rolled up his trouser legs and pointed to his shins where I'd rammed him with the wheelbarrow. They were purple, black and blue with bruising. I'd gone in way too hard on him.

'How'd that happen to your legs, Dirk?'

'Rescuing Isis; I banged them on a rock jutting out of the cliff,' lied my twin with a straight face. It struck me hard, this was the first time I'd ever heard Dirk tell a deliberate lie, even to wind up someone on the yard.

As Dirk drew breath to elaborate the lie further, Shane stomped across with a big pair of sour eyes and a bellyaching face on him. He shoved Wart Boy in the chest with one hand and squeezed his face with the other.

'Leave him alone,' I threatened Shane, 'or I'll give you a leftover helping from last December!'

But Shane ignored me completely and, with both hands, grabbed Warren by the collar. Shane hissed in his face, 'So you're sniding off with Dirk and Ellie now, are you?' Shane dropped Wart Boy and shouted, 'Well snide off with them, you steaming bag of horse manure. See if I care!' He then turned on us. 'I hope you catch warts off him ... warts all over your ugly pigging faces.' And with that, Shane ran off, leaving Wart Boy following us around the yard.

'Dirk? Ellie? Can I hang around with you two?'

Dirk looked closely at Wart Boy, smiled at him and said, 'Warren, if you and me were the last people alive on the earth, I'd go off and play on my own.' Dirk laughed in his face and told him, 'Go and bug somebody else, Wart Boy!'

I didn't say anything to Dirk; there seemed no point. But being around him was beginning to feel weirder by the hour. I tried to ignore it, I tried to pretend it was just my imagination but the truth was this: more and more, Dirk just didn't sound like Dirk anymore.

Chapter 24

'C'mon, Dirk,' I said, as we left the school gates. 'I'll treat you to a Pepsi Max and an hour on the Internet!' We turned in the direction of the town centre, where it felt like the sea was sucking whatever warmth there was in the air and replacing it with vast waves of cold.

'Where'd you get the money to go to Cyberspace Café?' asked Dirk.

'M um, she gave me money without me even asking. Last night.' It was completely out of the blue, and made me think something was going on with her and Dad.

Dirk's face lit up as we went into Cyberspace, and I told him, 'We've got enough for two Pepsi Maxes and an hour on the "net".'

'Are we going on Cartoon Network?'

'After we've found what I'm looking for.'

'Half an hour on Cartoon Network first!'

'It's my money, Dirk! Shall I see you back at the house?'

He stepped back and nodded. He had no choice in the matter. 'OK,' he said.

We settled at the computer with our drinks and a strong warning that if we spilled our drinks on the computer we'd have to pay to replace the damaged equipment.

'What are we looking for?' asked Dirk.

'Information about the past,' I told him. About Mrs Nijinsky's past, I thought. One way, I'd learned, to stop feeling worried about or scared of a situation was to find out as much as possible.

I typed 'Google' into the search engine and when the Google page showed on screen, I typed 'Hexhill-on-Sea' on the Google engine and waited.

Three matches were found, one, two, three in rich blue writing. The first match was no good, it was about a place called Hexhill-on-Sea in New Zealand. The second match was Hexhill-on-Sea's town council website. But the third match made my toes tingle.

HEXHILL-ON-SEA. A history of its lighthouse.

I clicked on and the blue writing turned purple as it downloaded onto the computer. My eyes stroked the screen. Hexhill-on-Sea had its first lighthouse during the time of Henry VIII. I clicked on the scrollbar and scrolled down through the unfolding centuries, seventeeth, eighteenth, nineteenth, the reign of Queen Victoria.

I stopped scrolling as I hit an onscreen black and white photograph of a man and a woman and a baby girl.

The caption underneath the photograph read: 'Amos and Rachel Moses and their daughter Miriam, 1903.'

The subheading read: 'The story of the last Lighthouse Keeper in Hexhill-on-Sea'.

'What's it say, Ellie? What's it say?'

'I'll tell you when I've read it.'

'Who's that baby? Is that baby, Mrs Nijinsky?' he persisted in my ear.

'Yeah!' I shouted, gathering surprised glances from all around. 'Yeah, that's her, now let me read the info.'

There was three pages of it, and another photograph of

Miriam, aged 14, and her father Amos, just before he died, in 1916.

It was weird, you could tell it was Mrs Nijinsky at a glance, even though she was young and very pretty with a bundle of thick brown hair. Her father, holding a Bible, looked severe, like he'd never cracked a smile in his entire life.

'What's it say, Ellie? What's it say?'

'It says, Dirk, that Mrs Nijinsky's name used to be Miriam Moses. She was an only child because her mum died of influenza in 1903. She grew up in the lighthouse with her dad who was a very, very religious man. In fact he was so religious that he used to go into Hexhill town and preach the gospel on the streets, shouting at the top of his voice that the whole town was going straight down to Hell because the people were sinful wretches who turned their backs on God. Hellfire and agony, he promised them, when they died, as they walked by and laughed in his face. He was so religious that he wouldn't let Miriam out of the lighthouse on her own. The only time she ever saw other people was when she was standing on the street with her dad screaming that the Devil was waiting with outstretched arms to drag them down to the fires of Hell. They used to call him the Mad Preacher.

'Then, in 1916, in World War I, there was a terrible storm at sea. Miriam's dad went out in a boat and drowned. Miriam said they'd seen a distress signal from a boat. Miriam nearly drowned trying to rescue him. The Council closed the lighthouse down and Miriam was turned out onto the street. She left Hexhill-on-Sea and was never seen again.'

I turned to Dirk, his face was blank.

'That's the story,' I said. 'What do you think?'

'I think I'd like to go on Cartoon Network now.'

Chapter 25

For days and nights on end, our house had been like a noise factory, so when we let ourselves in the silence hit me like a punch between the eyes.

'It's too quiet!' said Dirk, as Dempsey crept out of the living room with his chin almost brushing the carpet.

'What's going on, Dempsey?' I asked as he walked past us and curled up, shivering, on the bottom stair. The house felt cold, colder than the February afternoon should have made it feel, cold like the heating hadn't been on all day.

There were two messages on the telephone answering machine. Dirk pressed the replay button so we could listen back to them.

'Dirk...Ellie...' It was Charlie Chivers. 'It's Monday 9th February, half past nine in the morning. Mrs Nijinsky asked me to call and remind you that her birthday party's on Friday. She's getting very excited about reaching the grand old age of one hundred years...but she's getting even more excited about seeing the two of you and having you round for the evening.' Charlie stopped speaking but I knew the message wasn't over because I could still hear him breathing. 'No doubt we'll see the two of you before Friday but just to remind you. Farewell then, Ellie, and goodbye, Dirk!'

Farewell then, Ellie, and goodbye, Dirk! There was something in the way he said this that made me go cold in the armpits. Not that I had time to worry about it because the next message piped out.

There was a lot of background noise; it was a railway station by the sound of it and whoever was calling was on a pay phone. There was a lot of muttering, like the receiver was muffled by a hand and then, 'Dirk! Ellie!' It was Mum.

Dirk looked at me and I looked at him and I could tell we were both thinking the same thing, that a nasty shock was coming over from the parent corner. 'Ellie!' She laughed falsely and cleared her throat. 'Listen, er . . . Your dad and me, we're going to be out of town for a while, not very long, only a couple of weeks. The thing is, we've been offered the chance of a lifetime. We've been offered a place on a tour of Europe, it's *The Punk Rock All Stars of Yesteryear Road Show* . . . there's us and a load of our old mates. I know you'll understand. We couldn't say, "No!" Now, listen, listen, very carefully. You mustn't tell anyone we've left you in the house on your own, so if anyone asks where we are tell them we're ill in bed or we'll be back in an hour, use your imaginations. OK? OK! The other thing's this. There's enough food in the house to keep you going for a few days. We'll send you enough money to keep going, we're going to be so, so, so rich when this tour's over!'

This explained yesterday's outburst of generosity.

Dad's voice cut across Mum's. 'Come on, Hazel, hang up, we're going to miss the train.' He sounded in a great big hurry. Mum carried on, 'Listen, I've just *got* to go now. The thing is, Dad and me, we love you loads. But keep your traps shut. OK!' And with that the line went dead and the message ended.

Dirk sat down on the floor, stroking Dempsey and staring into space. 'Why don't they want us to say anything?' he asked.

'Because it's against the law to leave kids of our age on our own. They could get sent to jail for it.'

A smile thawed out the vacant look on Dirk's face. 'So we can drop them in it with the police when they get back then?' Dirk spoke his thought aloud.

'Dirk!' I was shocked. 'You're not serious.'

'So long as they do what we say, they stay out of jail!'

'Hey, Dirk, you're not seriously suggesting we blackmail our own mum and dad?'

'Why not?' Dirk replied. '*They* don't give a hoot about us! Anyway, we can always go and stay with Mrs Nijinsky and Charlie Chivers.' Dirk was running up the stairs going up them three steps at a time. 'Maybe they'd adopt us and we could get driven round in the limo all day long.'

I looked at Dempsey who stared up at me with a look of confusion.

'I'd rather live under the same roof as Shane Sharples,' I hissed, 'than go and live with that pair of ...'

'I'm serious!' Dirk looked over the stairs at me. 'Mrs Nijinsky'd take us in.'

'But what about Dempsey, Dirk?' I asked, reminding him. 'You told me she didn't like animals.'

'Well ... I guess we'd just have to get rid of Dempsey. Sell him or get him put down or something like that.'

Dempsey jumped up and ran to the back of the house. Dirk sang happily and at the top of his voice as he slammed the bathroom door shut after himself. I walked up the stairs, shouting, 'Dirk? What's got into you?'

But he turned both taps on and raised the volume on his singing. So I banged on the bathroom door. And he flushed the toilet. And sang just a little louder until I stopped banging and went back downstairs to feed Dempsey and try to stop my head from caving in.

TUESDAY 10th FEBRUARY

Chapter 26

'What's the matter with you two?' Miss Harper asked, forcing Dirk and me to line up together so we'd be sure to sit with each other near the front of the line for that special assembly.

'Nothing, Miss,' I answered as we marched down the corridor towards the hall.

'Fifty quid, eh?' she smacked her lips together. 'You'll be able to buy yourself another sleigh . . . '

'I don't think so, Miss!'

'So what will you do with the money? Any ideas?' It seemed clear to me that Miss Harper had taken a whole bottle of nosy cow tablets.

'No idea, Miss. Give it away to charity, maybe, Miss!' I snapped.

'I was only asking, Eleanor.' Which is what she called me when she was narked.

Mr Slater was sitting with the teachers, smiling like the King of the Heap and holding a white envelope in his hand. I wanted to jump up and tell him to keep the fifty but the hall was already full of kids and teachers and it was just too late for that. Mrs Miles was getting the school camera out of its black case and loading a new film into the back. Mr Spanner stepped forward and, with a wave of the hand, called us out in front of the whole silent school.

'The heroes of the hour, Dirk and Eleanor Beckett . . . '

I tried not to listen to anymore, as Spanner blathered on. I looked around as he went on and on and on. 'They saved the cat's life!' he told the hushed hall. 'The vet said Isis was desperate for a drink, was at death's door.' He smiled at us, his baldy head twinkling beneath the tortured thatch in the fluorescent light. 'Mr Slater, step forward with the reward please ... '

Mr Slater stepped between us and extended his arm. Dirk shook hands with him and then I did and then Mr Slater handed the white envelope to me.

'Worth every last penny it is,' he said. Mrs Miles took a picture in a blinding flare of flashlight and the envelope was thrust into my hand.

'Say thank you, Ellie,' Dirk whispered.

'Thanks ... thank you, Mr Slater ... can I sit down now?' I came over all dizzy, like I was going to faint, felt the floor wobble at my toes and the ceiling, roof and sky press down on the crown of my scalp. I walked back and just about made it to my place in line. I was sweating and Mrs Miles didn't help matters by bending right over me and cutting out the air supply. 'Are you all right, Eleanor?' she asked.

'Yeah,' I lied. 'I guess it's all a bit much, a bit much ... this excitement ... ' And then everything went jet black and dead silent.

I woke up in the medical room, on the bed in the corner with Miss Harper holding my hand and Dirk sitting on a chair looking at me. He held up the white envelope and said, 'Don't panic, Ell, I've got the money!'

'You fainted in the hall, Ellie,' Miss Harper said,

stating the flaming obvious.

'What time is it?' I asked.

'Twenty to four,' she answered.

I sat up immediately and said, 'Hometime!' But Miss Harper laid a hand on my shoulder and said, 'I've tried to phone your home, but your mum and dad are out. Do you know where they are?'

Dirk smiled behind her back and coldly said, 'Mum and Dad've left us all on our own and gone abroad!'

'Don't be silly, Dirk,' she replied.

'Yeah. Only kidding, Miss,' Dirk sighed.

'They've gone to visit a sick aunt. They'll be back at six o'clock,' I lied, standing up.

'I'll give you a lift home in the car,' Miss Harper offered, but I stood my ground and shook my head.

'The fresh air'll do me good ... '

'Are you sure?' she asked.

'I'd like to go home now, Miss. Come on, Dirk. Let's get going ... '

It was cold enough to freeze the spit in your mouth. When we saw the bus coming we ran to the stop and made our way to the warmest place we knew, the back seat, and sat shivering and shaking like a pair of abominable snowmen looking for a quick thaw.

'Are you OK, Ellie?' Dirk asked, sounding like the Dirk I thought I knew so well but would never see or hear again.

'I'm OK.'

'I'll make you a hot drink when we get in,' he said.

'That'd be nice, Dirk. We'll get the chippy for our tea.'

I smiled. It all started to feel all right again, like it used to.

Dirk showed me the white envelope and whispered, 'We'll be able to buy everything on the menu board.'

I took the envelope from Dirk and tore it open along the top edge with the tip of our front door key. The brown note glided out of the envelope onto my lap and if I hadn't been so shocked by what I saw, I'd have screamed so loud the bus would have crashed. The Queen's eyes were covered by a pair of dark blue ink blots. Was it the exact same £50 note that had slipped from the Jinx's hand?

'That's a coincidence,' muttered Dirk, totally unbothered. 'It looks like the money Mrs Nijinsky dropped, the money you stole from her, Ellie!'

'We stole, Dirk, you and me . . .'

I turned it over. Sir Christopher Wren had the bubble coming from his mouth and the words, *My name is Wren but I cannot fly*, written inside the bubble.

It was definitely *the* £50 note. It filled me with horror but I couldn't take my eyes off it.

'What's that?' asked Dirk, pointing at a string of letters and numbers printed along the edge of the note.

'It's the serial number,' I said.

'DB 11 31 10 90!' Dirk read it out loud, and again, 'DB 11 31 10 90! Hey, DB, my initials, and I'm 11 years old.'

'It's even got your birth date on it, Dirk! 31st day of the 10th month – October – 90, which is 1990.'

Dirk snatched the note up and examined the serial number. 'Oh yeah!'

'We'll give it back to the Jinx and then we'll be all even

with her, we won't have anything more to do with her then, we'll be – it'll be like none of this had ever happened...'

I was speaking very quickly but Dirk was staring at the £50 bank note, turning it this way and that and saying, 'My initials! My birth date! How about that then?'

'Are you two staying there all night or what?' The driver got out of his seat down at the front and looked up the long aisle at us. We'd long gone past our stop, we'd arrived at the bus station at the edge of town. 'Off you get!' he ordered, pointing at the door. Dirk clutched the £50 note in his fist and started making his way down the aisle. 'How about that? How about that?' he muttered.

'Dirk, we'll give the money back, we'll go round now and post it through the letterbox and never go back there again.'

He walked off the bus, his strides growing longer, his step getting quicker and I hurried to catch him up. Dirk wasn't listening, he was lost in some other world that I just couldn't get into.

There was a large arch that led out of the bus station onto the street, a large arch that was drowned in shimmering shadows and yellow sodium street lights.

'Charles!' Dirk called out. But there was no one around. 'Mr Chivers!' Dirk cried, as he broke into a run, towards the arch.

The front end of the white limousine nosed into the arch, its headlights picking up a band of pale mist that curled around the pavement and street. Soon the whole body of the car blocked the gap and the back door opened wide just as Dirk got there.

'Don't get in, Dirk!' I shouted, my feet glued to the ground by fear. 'Please!'

But he just turned around, calm as a courgette in a cool box, and called back, 'Come on, Ellie, let's go!'

For a moment, he waited for me and I waited for him and then he stepped inside the limousine. The door he'd disappeared behind closed and the car went away, suddenly vanished like some invisible rubber had swiped it clean off the street like a pencil smudge on a snow white page.

'Dirk!' I shouted his name louder than I'd ever shouted anything in my life, and the sound came back at me as a hollow echo. I ran out of the bus station and saw the tail end of the limo and its rear lights disappearing into the thickening fog.

'Dirk!' I called his name again and felt the darkness gathering in the sky leak into my ears and nose and eyes.

'Dirk?' I whispered, like I'd just woken up in hospital and found I'd had my arms surgically removed.

'Dirk?'

Alone, I began the long walk home, with a sudden and disturbing thought. Dirk was a puppet and Charlie Chivers was pulling all the strings.

Chapter 27

I was alone, and I was dead scared in the house. So I turned on all the lights in all the rooms and, armed with a baseball bat, opened every cupboard and closet door there was. I looked under all the tables and chairs downstairs and, up the shadow-heavy stairs, beneath each and every bed and wardrobe. Dempsey must've picked up my spooked-out vibes because I found him hiding in my room, trying to squeeze his bulk through the ten-centimetre gap between my bed and the floor. Dempsey was shaking like he'd been pumped full of jagged ice. I dragged him out and threw my arms around him for a long, long time.

When I was sure in my own mind that no one was lurking, I turned off the lights in Dirk's room and, with his binoculars, headed for the window.

There were lights on in the windows of the Jinx's lighthouse and even though I was scared for myself where I was, I was more scared for Dirk over there. *No one made him get into the car and go there*, a voice inside me said. *He wanted to go*, I reminded myself. *But Dirk*, I could never forget, *was blessed with the brains of a rocking horse and the good sense to match*.

Bam! There was a loud and sudden noise behind me and the surface of my scalp tightened with fear; it was a book fallen from Dirk's bedside table and onto the floor.

I could feel my heartbeat in the back of my teeth as I stooped to pick it up, *Greek Myths and Legends*, the book the Jinx had given him, open at the story of Icarus the boy who flew off the island with his dad, the page I heard Dirk read to her.

I took it to my room (where I'd stocked up with a loaf, some chocolate and a bottle of Pepsi Max), and jamming a chair against the door handle I turned to Dempsey and said, 'Let's see what happens next to Icarus.'

So I lay down on the bed and read the rest of the story.

It all seemed to be going well for Icarus and his dad. They strapped on the wings and flew off the island. Icarus was edgy at first, as the space between his toes and the sloshing sea below grew vaster, but the further away they flew, the more the fear drained out of Icarus. The higher he started flying, turning figures of eight in the sunshine and laughing like a symphony of exploding paper bags, the easier he felt with the thin air around him. Icarus's dad warned him not to fly too high because of the heat of the sun. Icarus's dad warned him that the heat of the sun would melt the wax off his wings if he flew too near it. But Icarus didn't listen.

Icarus flew too near the sun. The wings melted away from him and he fell down to earth like a person chucked out of an aeroplane without a parachute.

I closed the book and felt certain of one thing. I had to get Dirk away from Chivers and the Jinx.

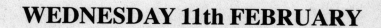
WEDNESDAY 11th FEBRUARY

Chapter 28

'Dirk Beckett!' Miss Harper called his name from the morning register but he wasn't in school. 'Ellie?' she carried on.

'Yes, Miss?'

'Where's Dirk?'

'He's not been very well. He was in bed when I left the house...asleep—'

Just as I was about to start dressing up the lie in a few colourful details, the classroom door opened and Dirk walked in, the healthiest, happiest looking kid in town.

'Feeling well all of a sudden, are we?' asked Miss Harper.

'Never better, Miss Harper,' he replied.

'What's going on, Eleanor?' She dropped her pen and drilled my face from the roots of her eyeballs.

'I stayed in bed an extra half hour,' Dirk rescued me from the hole. 'I wasn't feeling right but the extra nap's fixed me up.' He was getting really good at telling lies.

She carried on with the register and I smiled at Dirk but he looked right through me as though I didn't exist. As he burrowed in his desk for his Maths folder, I felt really sad, like I didn't have a brother anymore, like he'd forgotten all about me, like all the years we'd spent together had been a dream he couldn't be bothered remembering and I could never have the heart to forget.

I deliberately snapped the end of my pencil and made my way over to where Dirk was sitting. 'Borrow your pencil sharpener?' I asked, but he didn't look up, he just shoved it towards me. I picked it up. 'Dirk, we've got to talk...' He didn't even lift his eyes. 'Don't go back to Mrs Nijinsky's, stay in ours...'

'Look,' he hissed. 'I've got work to do. OK!' He wrote the day, *Wednesday* and the date, *11/2* in the neatest, clearest writing I'd ever seen him do. He had his own special folder of Maths work, simple sums from which he pulled a sheet of laughably easy addition work.

'I'll help you!' I offered.

'I don't need help!' And finally, he looked at me. 'I can manage on my own. Sit down, let me get on with my own work, just go away!'

So I did just that.

At lunch time, there was a snarl-up in the girls' toilets because someone had blocked up the loos with bean bags, and when I finally got into the hall, Shane was in my place at the packed lunch table, laughing and joking with Dirk. 'You're in my place!' I told him, fighting down the urge to smash him about the head with my lunch box.

Dirk pointed down the table where there was an empty space at the end. 'There's a place down there for you!' He turned and smiled at Shane and said, 'Go on, Shane, what were you saying?'

As I walked away, Shane whispered something and Dirk's laughter roared after me to the end of the row. I decided to ignore him for the rest of the day but if it meant pinning him down to the playground at hometime and threatening him with the kicking of his lifetime, he was coming back to the house with me.

Chapter 29

At the end of the day, Dirk's face was the first one out onto the yard. Mine was number two. I tailed after him and in all the chaos of mums and dads, the dogs on leads and babies in buggies, I lost him straight away. I looked to a hundred places in a handful of moments as I hurried to the main gate but there was no Dirk. I turned a full circle on the spot and caught a glimpse of his head bobbing out of sight, as he turned the corner to the back end of the school. I took to my toes and made it after him, turning the corner, calling out, 'Dirk!' and . . . he wasn't there.

Isis wandered out of Slater's shed but there was no other movement. I ducked my head down and ran as quickly as I could past the back of the kitchen and the bins and froze when I heard him say, '*Ellie!*' like he'd appeared from nowhere, just behind me. I turned and looked up. The boiler house had a low flat roof, and Dirk was crouched on the edge looking down at me. 'Ellie!'

'How are things, Dirk?' I asked, stepping back to get a better view of him. The moon was forming in the sky behind his head.

'I think you've upset Mrs Nijinsky, Ellie,' he told me. 'And Mr Chivers.'

'How?' I asked.

'You wouldn't come with me last night. She was angry.

But he said you were a bad influence on me. Mr Chivers said I was a nice boy but you . . . you're a thief, Ellie!'

I opened my mouth to argue, to defend myself but remembered the £50 note and said, 'I made a mistake, Dirk. One mistake. And you had fun that day spending the money, you joined in, remember.'

'But I wanted to give it back to Mrs Nijinsky, outside the post office . . .'

'So she knew all along,' I said, feeling deeply and horribly freaked all of a sudden. 'What did she say about you, Dirk? Tell me more.'

'She said I was a good boy for bringing back the fifty quid!'

The way he said this and the look in his eyes made me sick with anger.

'Just hang on,' I said. 'I wanted to take that money back, remember. *Post it through the letterbox*, I said. You were all for blowing it down at the chip shop! Remember?'

But Dirk just laughed at me and shook his head as if I was the one getting things all mixed up.

'How did she know about the fifty quid? Did she tell you, Dirk? How did she know it was me didn't hand it back?'

'I didn't say that much,' said Dirk. 'She seemed to know anyway. She seems to know everything.'

'You told her it was me?' I couldn't believe it. 'Dirk?' Dirk had snitched on me, totally and utterly ratted on me. I stared at him. I wanted to kill him there and then. He smiled and looked directly at me.

'She knew already...' Dirk announced, standing to his full height, on his tiptoes, on the very edge of the boiler house roof.

'Get down, Dirk! Get down now, and come back to the house with me!'

But he smiled and smiled and smiled and replied, 'No. You come with me!' He stretched his arms out, like he was trying to balance himself. 'Ellie, she said she'll forgive you...if you only come to the house...and say, "*Sorry, Mrs Nijinsky!*"'

'Sorry?' I spat it out. 'I'm sorry I ever clapped eyes on the old bag but no, Dirk. I'm never going back there again. And I don't want you going there either.' Dirk bent his arms at the elbow and started moving them in a wide figure of eight. 'She said, Ellie, you're still welcome to come to her birthday party on Friday. Mr Chivers is making a huge cake. Come with me, Ellie, come with me now. Come with me...and fly!'

Dirk jumped up and away from the boiler house roof, in a long elegant leap that ended with him falling onto his feet, hitting the tarmac with a cry of delight; he didn't stop but carried on running and howling with laughter like he wasn't quite right in the head. He slipped through a cluster of conker trees beyond which was a gap in the railings. A few seconds later, when I chased after him through the trees, Dirk was gone.

Chapter 30

I took out my key. When I pressed it against the lock with the lightest touch, the front door opened wide. I choked on a breath of cold air. I'd double checked and triple checked the door before leaving for school that morning.

The door was unlocked. Someone was either in there or had been in the house while I was at school.

'Mum? Dad?' I called. 'Are you back?' But there was no reply. 'Dempsey!' I yelled, as I stepped inside. 'Dempsey! Dempsey! Dempsey!' I bellowed. 'Come on, come here, boy!' Nothing. Not a woof or a whisper. I bounced through the house, pushing open doors as I passed them but there was no sign of anything being stolen. I got to the kitchen and Dempsey's breakfast was still in the bowl, his water tray untouched. 'Dempsey!' I was frantic. Dempsey was gone and... and the kitchen door was wide open and, outside, the garage door was rolled up. Maybe, I thought, maybe, I wished and hoped, Dempsey was in the garage.

I switched on the garage light but Dempsey wasn't there. But the grey dust sheets underneath which we'd hidden *that* sleigh were thrown in the corner and there was an empty space where it'd been. Dempsey was gone, the sleigh was gone. And whoever'd got into the house had used a key, whoever'd been in and snatched

Dempsey had been and used the house key and the only other person with a key was Dirk.

I sat down and took a few deep breaths. Dirk must've given his key to the Jinx and Charlie Chivers. They had Dempsey, up at her house, against the dog's will. They'd interfered with Dirk's brain somehow and that's why he was at the lighthouse, and they'd dognapped Dempsey. Enough was enough.

I took a torch and the baseball bat and found myself running through the streets towards the Jinx's place. There was a row of boarded-up shops not far from the top of our street and as I passed by I saw something that pulled me up and made the hair freeze on my head. The boards were covered in blown-up copies of the poster of Mum and Dad that Shane had brought into school and on each of the posters was a message: *Watch them on BBC 1...Friday, 13th February!* I flashed the torchlight across the posters and muttered, 'Why me?' Shane Sharples' laughing face came to my mind; this was his idea of fun, plastering Mum and Dad's punk picture about the place for the whole town to see, making sure no one forgot to watch them making fools of themselves on TV.

I switched the torch off and turned away. There were no lights on in Hexhill Lighthouse but I had the strangest feeling that inside, the Jinx and Chivers were sitting, watching me from one of the many windows.

I banged the boarded-up shop window hard with the baseball bat and tried to swallow my fear. I ran towards the clifftop path and as I ran I tried to think. Seeing as Isis had been trapped inside the air raid shelter in the back garden, that seemed like a good place to start looking for Dempsey.

There were shadows everywhere once I got past the open gates and I figured that if I stayed in the dark places, I could get round the side of the house and into the garden without a hitch. The grass squelched beneath my trainers and the wind made a weird hissing sound through the hedges but these weren't the sounds that made me stop.

There was a sound of something sharp cutting into rubber, grinding and scraping. I followed the noise, it was coming from the side of the limo. I couldn't believe my eyes. Dempsey was chewing one of the front tyres. Dempsey was so busy, so taken up with what he was doing that he didn't sense me standing and watching him.

'Dempsey!' I called softly, flashing the torch on and off to attract his attention.

'Oaof! Oaof!' It was a joy to hear him.

'Dempsey!' He jumped towards me as I dropped down to wrap my arms around him. His mouth and gums were raw and bleeding after chewing up the limo's tyres.

'Ssh, ssh, shush now, Dempsey! Be quiet . . . I wish you could tell me what's going on here.' But Dempsey was clearly agitated and, I could tell, wanted me to follow him into the garden. 'OK, Dempsey! Ssh, quietly, let's go . . . '

I stalked Dempsey down the garden path: I flashed the torch for half a second and lit up the air raid shelter. Dempsey stopped and looked up at me.

'What is it, Dempsey?' He looked right at the shelter and let out a low growl. Side by side, we stepped closer. The door was back up, blocking the entrance and, for a moment, I thought I heard a voice from inside. It was Dirk's voice.

'Dirk?' I took a step closer and listened.

'I want to fly, I can fly, I will fly.' Dirk was inside the shelter, talking like his brain had been meddled with. 'I want to fly, I can fly, I will fly...' He sounded like he was talking in his sleep. I dropped the torch and bat and grabbed the side of the door that blocked the shelter. Alone, it was like trying to move a brick wall. I heaved and strained with all I had, tuning in to Dirk, 'I want to fly, I can fly, I will fly...'

'Need any help there, Eleanor?' A single beam of torchlight shone into my eyes as I turned quickly to the voice and the light. It was Chivers and the old Jinx herself. 'You'll never move a big door like that on your own,' said Chivers.

'Not a young girl like you,' Jinxy remarked. The way they were looking at me through the light made my teeth tingle and my stomach knot.

'I've come for my brother and my dog. I want them back now, or else!'

'Or else!' Chivers let out a low thin whistle.

'Or else what, dear?' She turned to Chivers and shook her head.

'I know,' said Chivers, holding the baseball bat I'd just dropped. He smiled at me. 'Or else you'll hit us with your baseball bat?' He swung the bat back and aimed it at my head. 'Like this?'

The last thing I saw as I ducked away from the swing of the baseball bat, and bashed my head against the wall of the air raid shelter was Charlie Chivers' teeth, shining, his mouth opening into a wide grin. And the last thing I heard, as I slumped to the ground, was Mrs Nijinsky laughing, laughing, laughing.

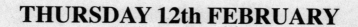

THURSDAY 12th FEBRUARY

Chapter 31

Somewhere, far away, a clock chimed midnight and from the deepest darkness around me a whole new day began. Slowly, I came round with a head that felt like it'd been bounced around a basketball court. Charlie Chivers and Mrs Nijinsky were clinking glasses together and laughing to themselves.

I lay as still as a chopped-down tree. I could feel them moving nearer to me, peering at me like I was an object on display in a museum.

'Maybe she hit her head a little too hard?' Mrs Nijinsky muttered.

'Or not quite hard enough, Mrs Nijinsky,' replied Charlie Chivers, with a grin in his voice. 'Not that it matters. She'll be dead inside twenty-four hours as it is!' Fear rippled through me and my teeth turned dry and cold, then sharp like ice daggers against my lips and tongue. There was a taste of blood, sweet and metallic in the back of my throat. *She'll be dead inside twenty-four hours!* It was all I could do not to scream.

'Her and Dirk, dead as a pair of dusty doornails.' Mrs Nijinsky clearly liked the idea.

'Deader, Mrs Nijinsky, deader even than a pair of dozy dinosaurs.'

I opened my eyes to slits and made out that I was in the kitchen of the lighthouse with Chivers and the Jinx now sitting in front of the fire and me lying on the table, so, so scared I hardly dared take breath for fear they'd hear me and finish me off there and then.

'So, Mr Chivers, how will *she* be killed?' Nijinsky asked.

'*She* shall be killed with kindness,' laughed Chivers. They seemed to find this very funny and every pot and pan in the kitchen shook, the glass in the window frames rattled and each bone in my body trembled as they snorted and wheezed with delight. I wanted to jump up and run away but instead I stayed so still I could have been dead already. *She shall be killed with kindness!* What was Chivers going to do? Offer me a slice of birthday cake laced with rat poison...

'And is Dirk good and ready to die?' Nijinsky asked.

'Oh yes, Dirk's all set to die!' Chivers told her, with a coldness creeping into his voice that made me open my eyes, slowly, slowly, little by little. 'Now, Mrs Nijinsky, it's time for you and me to get down to business. It's time to sign the deal.'

By the glow of the oven range, Chivers pulled out a rolled-up scroll from inside his long black butler's coat and a posh-looking ink pen, both of which he handed to the Jinx.

'Read it to me, my tired old eyes aren't what they were.'

'Aah, but they will be, they will be... once Dirk's dead and gone.' He cleared his throat and began to read. '"The agreement between Mrs Nijinsky and Mr Chivers to give Mrs Nijinsky an extra seventy years to live. On the morning of her one hundredth birthday, I, Mr Charles

Chivers, will give you, Mrs Nijinsky, seventy years to add on to the end of your life . . . " '

'Wait a minute, Mr Chivers,' said the Jinx. 'I think I saw the child move.' I clamped my eyes shut and willed myself to lie stiller than concrete.

'Oh, don't let her worry you, Mrs Nijinsky. There's a very easy way to tell if she's awake.'

There was a horrid noise of footsteps coming closer to me and Mrs Nijinsky asking, 'What are you doing, Mr Chivers?'

'I've got a red hot fire poker in my hand, a poker that's been heating up in the fire for hours and hours on end and I'm going to stick it right down on her face till it sizzles the skin on her cheeks to a crisp. That'll teach her to listen in on her elders and betters.'

I jumped up from the table and cried out, 'No! No, no, no! Don't do that! Don't burn me with the poker!'

'Fooled you,' said Chivers. There was no red hot poker, there was nothing at all in his hands. 'Well, you certainly fell for that one, Eleanor,' he laughed. 'Be warned! Don't even think of trying to escape, or *else*!'

Mrs Nijinsky was behind him now, staring at me with a cruel grin and chilly, fishy eyes. 'Don't move, Eleanor!' she ordered.

'Now,' Chivers said, twisting my ears sharply. 'Where were we?'

'Look, let me go!' I was talking too fast and too loudly. 'Let me and Dirk and Dempsey go and I promise you we won't say a word, I promise, please.' I was wasting words. The Jinx just laughed at me.

'Let you go?' she grinned. 'You don't understand, Eleanor. Explain it all to her, Mr Chivers.'

'It's like this,' Chivers told me. 'Dirk is Mrs Nijinsky's passport to an extra seventy years of life. We're doing a deal, Mrs Nijinsky and I. She gives me £1,000,000 and I give her an extra seventy years of life.'

It was plain from what he was saying that they were both raving mad. Or maybe, the Jinx was mad and Charlie Chivers was anything but mad. The way I was hearing it, Chivers was stripping her of a massive amount of money with some hocus pocus deal. I was amazed. She'd seemed so normal, so aware, and for a woman of ninety-nine years so unfuddled.

The tiny spot in my stomach where I felt all the good and bad things in this life twitched, as my insides turned upside down and back to front.

'But what's this deal of yours got to do with Dirk?' I asked.

'It's Dirk's seventy years I'm going to give to Mrs Nijinsky,' Chivers replied, quietly. 'Dirk's going to kill himself, he's going to throw his young life away, and I'm going to give all his years to Mrs Nijinsky.'

'Kill himself?' I echoed Chivers' words. 'Throw his life away?'

'That's right,' the Jinx chipped in. 'He's going to kill himself tomorrow morning, on my hundredth birthday.'

But, I thought, *but even if Dirk does die, Chivers can't take all those years and give them to Mrs Nijinsky like they were gift vouchers. If Dirk dies, his years go with him.*

'But . . . ' I said, thinking out loud.

'But what, Eleanor?' Chivers hissed.

'But nothing.' I stayed silent. Nijinsky obviously believed this deal was going to work but one thing was certain. Chivers had the power, the power over Mrs Nijinsky, the power over Dirk, and the power over me. Nijinsky and Chivers stared at me as this bitter butter sank into the warm crust of my brain and then they burst out laughing as I started crying.

'There, there, Eleanor,' Mrs Nijinksy mocked me. 'You do understand, you'll have to die as well as Dirk. You know too much. I'm sure you'll understand.' She squeezed my cheeks and added, 'You thieving little madam!'

'The thing is, Eleanor,' explained Chivers, 'I've put the idea in Dirk's head that he can fly. He really believes that he can do it and tomorrow, he's going to take off. It won't take long before he's a dead duck.' Chivers pressed his face close to mine, his breath cold and sour on my skin.

'How did you do this to him?' I asked. 'How did you make him *believe*?'

'You know how much he wants to fly,' replied Chivers. 'He wants therefore he believes. In this world, Ellie, there are those people like Dirk who I can stick my fingers into, and shape their minds like Plasticine. You, Ellie, are a nasty, hard-faced, mouthy, unbelieving, pain-in-the-backside person. Your mean little mind is a locked door to me. However . . . ' He smiled and pointed to the ground. 'Down, down, down to the depths he goes! And you, Eleanor, you'll be going with him.'

The Jinx rolled the scroll out on the table and Chivers told her, 'Just sign along the dotted line at the bottom.' As she scratched her name on the scroll, my eyes locked into Chivers' eyes.

'Who are you?' I asked him.

'Wouldn't you like to know, Eleanor Beckett!' he smiled.

'You're a hypnotist, aren't you?'

'Very good, Ellie. Such a good brain you have; what a waste of a young life.'

'You're a hypnotist and a conman . . .' I snapped.

'I am what I am,' he said. 'It's all over for you and your brother now anyway.' He gazed deeper into my eyes, like he was trying to deep fry my brain.

'You'll never hypnotise me, Chivers. The only people who can be hypnotised are the ones who want to be. Like Dirk, and . . . ' I jabbed a finger in the Jinx's direction, 'and that stupid old bitch.'

The Jinx blew on her signature and she handed the scroll to Chivers, saying, 'A deal's a deal and it's you two or me, Eleanor. Don't talk to me like that, *young lady.*'

'Two dead children and a piece of paper, that's not going to buy you extra years, Mrs Nijinsky.' My voice sounded squeaky and desperate but Mrs Nijinsky was listening and she looked perplexed, like I'd made a hairline crack in the concrete certainty of what she wanted to believe. Chivers looked at me, as he got between me and Nijinsky, a death threat in his eyes, the poker in his hand.

'One more word, Ellie,' he whispered, 'and I'll sizzle your skin.'

I fell silent and Mrs Nijinsky yawned. 'I'm going to bed,' she announced. 'Big day ahead and all that.'

With that, she shuffled out of the kitchen leaving me alone with Charlie Chivers. He lit a cigarette with the poker and blew a stream of smoke in my direction.

There was a silence, a long silence, a twisted silence and a graveyard stillness. He was staring at me as my tears dried up and stopped rolling down my face.

'Where did you meet her?' I asked.

'Cruise ship. I was the cabaret act, magic and hypnotism. Well done, by the way, that was a really perceptive guess.'

'When I called you hypnotist? Or conman?'

'Both.'

'Is that your real name, Charlie Chivers?'

'I've already told you too much.'

'Look, if you control her mind, why don't you just stiff her for the million and disappear. You don't have to do this, you don't have to kill us. Fraud's one thing, murder's just...' I couldn't, I just couldn't find a word that expressed how I felt.

'Well...I guess I do owe you an explanation. The thing about mind control is this. No mind is a blank canvas. It's full of all kinds of ideas and experiences and memories. When you mess with a person's mind, you've got to mess with the things they know, the things they want, the things they need. Haven't you worked it out yet, the big thing about Mrs Nijinsky?'

133

'No.'

'She's a killer. She killed her three husbands. And her father. She likes to kill. If her head was full of flowers then I'd be working some fantastic plan to do with the garden. But her whole life's revolved around murder.'

'How did she kill them?'

'Her father, she drowned. Husband number one, Mr Flynn, she suffocated with a pillow. Husband two, Mr Frost, he *fell* from a moving train. Mr Nijinsky, well, she set him on fire! And it always looked tragic and accidental.' Chivers waited while the news sank in. 'It's nothing personal, Ellie,' said Chivers, stubbing his cigarette out on the wall. 'You and your brother were in the wrong place at the wrong time.'

'If she's that hard-headed, that hard-hearted, how did she ever fall for your patter?' I asked. Chivers pointed to his own skull and said, 'Dirk, open. Ellie, shut. Mrs N, open.'

He jabbed me with the baseball bat and whispered, 'Just walk!'

Chapter 32

I was taken to the room at the top of the lighthouse and stayed wide awake watching the dreadful dawn break, and hoping that the new day, our last day on earth, wouldn't arrive. But arrive it did. There were seagulls gliding and hovering around the large window where the big light used to shine on the sea.

It was a bright day outside and a cold light fell through the glass. I got up from the floorboards, looked out at the clifftops and the sea. The ground below from the large garden gates was locked in a casing of ice to the clifftops; perfect, I thought, for sleighing...

Dirk and me were going to die for some crackpot deal between a dangerous old loonie and a greedy conman with no regard for human life.

There were noises outside the room. I turned and walked away from the window as the door opened and Dirk walked in with the Jinx and Chivers. The Jinx and Chivers hung back by the door as Dirk came across to me.

'Dirk?' I said. He was smiling at me, just like the old Dirk and I wondered if this was a dream or my imagination playing a trick on me.

'Ellie, I've come to say goodbye. I'm going...on Mrs Nijinsky's hundredth birthday.' I looked past Dirk for a moment, at the Jinx and Chivers who stood there watching like a pair of beady-eyed old vultures hanging around a heap of fresh fleshy bones.

'Dirk, listen to me, you're going to kill yourself.'

'Kill myself, Ellie? I'm going to fly, that's what I'm going to do.' He pointed behind himself. 'They've given me the gift of flight.'

'Good boy,' Nijinsky egged him on. 'You tell her, Dirk.'

'Birds fly, Dirk. Bats fly, bees fly, butterflies fly, even flies fly but boys can't fly, Dirk!'

'You're talking in riddles, Ellie.'

'Say it to me, Dirk. Birds fly, bats fly, bees fly, butterflies fly, even flies fly but *boys can't fly*!'

'No, Ellie!' He shook his head, like I was the one who didn't understand properly. 'Those who believe they can fly, and who have the gift of flight, they fly!'

'It's a trick, Dirk. A dirty trick to kill you. I don't know what he's said or done to your brain but you'll end up in a coffin...'

But he just wasn't listening to me.

'Ellie, I'm going now. I don't know where I'm flying to or if I'll ever fly back again so I wanted to say goodbye to you. And thanks for all the times you stood up for me at school and in the street. And for all the times you helped with my reading. You've been a good sister to me. Thanks, Ellie, and goodbye.'

He was away, through the door and out, before I had the chance to beg him to stay. The room darkened over as I waited for either Chivers or Nijinsky to speak while outside, the bright day turned dark and overcast. Shadows stroked the walls and darkness sighed about my head. All I could see were her eyes. Chivers was no longer in the room. It was just me and her.

'Eleanor!' Mrs Nijinsky whispered at long last in a voice that was softer, different, like she'd decided, after all the horror, suddenly to be nice to me. 'Eleanor, it doesn't have to be like this. It doesn't have to be the end for you as well as for Dirk. I'm a lonely old woman and there's nothing I'd like more than the company of a bright young girl like you. I'm leaving here soon, Eleanor, and I'd like to take you with me, to be my friend and companion, to live a life of luxury. I've got more money than you can count in a thousand years, Eleanor. Come with me. We'll go everywhere and see everything. How does that sound to you, Eleanor? It's better than dying, and that's your only other option.'

'You didn't tell me, Mrs Nijinsky, that you'd killed your husbands and your dad.'

She shrugged, and smiled a smile that said, *'Silly old me and so what?'*

'Men have a habit of getting under the feet, dear. Sometimes, you have to give matters a little push in the direction you want them to go. How many times have you been in trouble because of Dirk? How many times have you wished you could be free to just get on with your life? You're here now because of him.'

It was totally dark in the room but I could still see her eyes glinting in the last wisps of a red sunset. What had happened to the daytime? What had happened to time?

'Don't worry about Dirk,' she told me. 'Tomorrow, he'll have his moment of glory, his moments in the air . . . '

'But he's going to die, isn't he? Tomorrow, Dirk will

die, won't he?'

The room was utterly silent and for a moment I pictured myself riding in the back of the limo, wearing the most expensive trainers in the world and holding my very own mobile phone on which I could order anything I wanted in the whole world. It felt good. It felt very, very good, but at the same time I was shocked and sickened at myself for even thinking like this.

'All you have to do is say, "*Yes!*"' she breathed. 'Come with me, you'd mean more to me than the world,' said Nijinsky.

I stared into her face and it looked exactly the way it did when we first called at the lighthouse.

'How can I trust a word you say?' I whispered into her eyes. 'You stroked Dempsey with one hand and fed him with the other but you hate animals. You were pretending to like Dempsey then just like you're pretending to like me now. I won't be your human dog. You're on your own, Nijinsky!'

As my words sank in and the softness lifted from her face, something I'd never seen before, something strange drifted into her eyes and settled there.

It was the indelible print of fear. I looked into her eyes and saw that inside her there was a growing sense of desperation and terror.

'Mrs Nijinsky, are you lonely?'

'I didn't have a little girl of my own,' she began. *It's no wonder*, I thought. *You stiffed your husbands before they had a chance to give you a baby.* 'With you, Eleanor, I wouldn't be lonely.' I held my hands out to her and she

138

took them. I delved into her eyes and she held my gaze.

'Miriam, what's the matter?' She blinked once, twice. 'What are you scared of, Miriam?' I asked. Her bony fingers squeezed my hands, like she was drowning and clinging on to me for life itself.

'I'm not afraid of dying, my dear. But …' A blue bloom flushed on her trembling lips, the wrinkled lines around her mouth shaping into a cobweb of fear. She couldn't speak, so I spoke the words for her.

'You're frightened about what's going to happen after you die,' I whispered her secret and she nodded slowly.

'Four murders, one of them my own father.' For the briefest moment, her face changed, and I saw her as a little girl, Miriam Moses, the lighthouse keeper's daughter. 'The Devil's waiting, just around the corner from this life, with outstretched arms, waiting to drag me into the fires of Hell for the rest of time.'

My head danced, my stomach gridlocked. This was it, this was the bottom line.

She believed she was damned, she had a one-way ticket to Hell and she'd do anything to put off the day she had to get on the train.

'What about Dirk? What will happen to him, Mrs Nijinsky? You can save his life.'

All the softness left her face. 'Tomorrow, Dirk will die!'

'Mrs Nijinsky, go and rot in Hell!'

'Have it your way, Eleanor!' She spat the words at me. 'You're a very stupid girl.'

'You're a long time dead, lady!' I snarled back at her.

I turned away and she left the room.

FRIDAY 13th FEBRUARY

Chapter 33

'It's your last chance, Ellie!' Chivers stood in the doorway and jangled the keys to the limo under my nose. 'Are you going to take Mrs Nijinsky's kind and generous offer or not?' It was early in the morning and outside I could hear Dempsey running round on the ice and barking against the cold.

'If I don't go with her, are you going to kill me?' I asked.

'No, Eleanor, you're a *real* fool. So I'll leave that job to you.'

'Then you'll be waiting a long, long time. You can't brainwash me like you've brainwashed Dirk.'

He yawned, 'Mrs Nijinsky's waiting outside in the car right now. You'll never have another chance like this. She's offering you a life of everything you ever wanted and more. Otherwise, you'll surely die. You can be saved. Dirk is enough for her. The choice is yours.'

'Everything I want,' I said, 'except Dirk alive and well. She can keep her fancy car, she can keep her money. Wherever you're going, I hope you have a fatal accident, I hope you crash the limo, I hope your brakes fail. Tell her from me, the answer's *no*!'

And without a further word, Chivers left the room... and left the door wide open. I walked over, very cautiously, expecting some trick or other but there didn't seem to be any. Through the door was a narrow winding

143

stone staircase that led all the way down the lighthouse. I looked over the handrail, down the drop in the middle – it was a long, long way down. I saw Chivers' grey head and his coat tails flapping behind him as he rushed away, round corner after corner.

'Chivers,' I called out. 'You've left the door open!'

Chivers stopped and looked up. 'You're really not as smart as you think you are. You should have checked the door. It was never locked!'

I ran after him, down the grey stone stairs, my running footsteps echoing after his laughter, my heart beating out a crazy rhythm inside me. I wanted to catch up with Chivers but every time I thought I was just one turn of the staircase away from him, he'd disappear from view and I'd see him three turns of the staircase away from me.

'Have a look from the window to your right!' His hollowed-out voice drifted up to me. I stopped and glanced out of a long narrow window. 'Dirk!' I cried as loudly as I could but he couldn't hear me.

Dirk was riding on the sleigh, skating down the icy slope from the garden gates to the clifftop with Dempsey running after him and barking for him to stop. I covered my eyes as he picked up speed. He was heading, one way and non-stop, to the very edge and there was nothing in the way to stop him. The faster the sleigh skidded towards the cliff edge, the more Dirk seemed to enjoy it, the louder he screamed with delight and happiness. I peeked through the gaps between my fingers and listened to the sound of Dirk laughing like a mad thing, having the time of his life as he hurtled towards his death.

Dirk was only seconds away from the edge of the cliff when he fluked out in the biggest way ever. I let out a tiny gasp as the sleigh reared up at the front and twisted over on itself and backwards, sending Dirk into a sidelong somersault which seemed to make him happier still. I hurried down the stairs, thinking the sleigh must have hit a heavy lump in the ground or a snowed-over boulder sticking out from the clifftop path.

As I ran out of the lighthouse, Chivers disappeared inside the limo. The car sped away through the open gates at the bottom of the garden. I followed in the tyre tracks left by the limousine which made it easier to run than on a slippery surface. Chivers and Nijinsky were heading along the road leading away from town, the road that ran parallel and alongside the clifftop.

Dirk was already on his feet and flapping his arms. He was way too near the edge of the cliff. I chased down the slope towards him. 'Dirk!' I called. He stopped what he was doing and turned, as I skidded and fell and got up and ran and skated and scraped my way down the slope.

'Stay right there, Dirk!'

'Come on, Ellie! Come on, come and fly with me!'

Dempsey struggled back up the slope, taking three steps forward and sliding back two as his front legs failed to support the weight of his rear end. 'Dirk, stay right where you are, OK!' I fixed my eyes on the sleigh which lay on its side as Dirk grinned and took two more paces to the edge of the cliff and looked over – a sight that would normally have had him screaming with terror. Instead, he chuckled and said, 'I'm so high up and it's so far down. The waves look like swirling foam in a bubble bath.'

I reached the sleigh and grabbed it with both hands. 'Dirk, reach out, take the end of the sleigh I'm holding out for you and come here where it's a bit safer.'

I grabbed Dempsey's collar and shouted in his face. 'Go and get some help!' He looked right into my eyes, blankly, confused even. I smacked his butt with the flat of my hand and yelled, 'Go!' He yelped, turned and hurtled out of the garden.

Dirk smiled at me and said, 'I'm going to fly now. Hold my hand and I'll take you with me! No? You won't come with me, Ellie?'

He extended his arms and bent his elbows.

He balanced on one foot, right on the very edge.

He was losing his balance, falling forwards over the cliff, arms flapping wildly as his foothold finally gave way to the weight of his body dropping off the edge . . . and there was nothing at all I could do.

He was laughing as he lost control, laughing as he went over and out of sight but, as soon as he was gone, a weird silence fell around us. And then . . .

He screamed at the top of his voice and cried, 'Ellie, Ellie, Ellie, help me, Ellie!'

I dragged the sleigh to the edge, for something to hold onto, and looked down where Dirk was splashing around in the water, with the waves tossing him about like he was a piece of driftwood. Dirk's brain must have stopped working from Chivers' trickery as soon as his life started flashing before him. Because even in the baby pool of Hexhill Leisure Centre, Dirk couldn't swim. He wouldn't even get into the baby pool without a swimming float.

'Oh, Dirk!' I screamed. 'What can I do?' Just looking over the edge made me feel dizzy and ill but seeing Dirk going down under the waves, his wild waving arms doing nothing to keep himself afloat made me shake with terror for him. I lifted the sleigh in both hands and felt the urge to smash it up when I suddenly felt my brain turn inside out with a sudden and brilliant idea. *He wouldn't even get in without a swimming float!*

Float, float, float, float! The word banged around my brain. I had both hands on the sleigh. It was strong enough to take both our weights yet light enough to lift up easily. The sleigh was as good as a float for people who couldn't swim.

I stood up and tried not to think, tried to move as quickly as I could before I had a chance to get scared witless. 'Dirk, hang on!' I stood on the edge. I didn't look down. I hung onto the sleigh. I jumped. I couldn't breathe in the few seconds that it took for me to fall all the way into the sea. I trapped the breath inside me and kept my eyes shut, feeling the darkness and the silence of the water as I sank beneath the cold surface. And in the silence, beneath the waves, I thought I heard the sound of Chivers and Nijinsky laughing and whispering, 'Kind to Dirk? Kindness, Eleanor, you're killing yourself with kindness!'

I gripped the sleigh and bounced up through the water on a powerful upthrust, popping out of the sea like a soggy and scared jack-in-the-box. And as I came up, I saw Dirk sink under, his head vanishing, his arms flying this way and that, the air leaving his lungs in great big bubbleloads. I grabbed one of his hands and curled his fingers around the edge of the sleigh. I grabbed his other arm and tugged him as hard as I could.

His head sprang from the water as he held on with both hands to the sleigh.

'Imagine you're holding onto the bar at the baths, Dirk! Just try and relax, and kick your legs gently.' He was crying and coughing because he'd swallowed a load of salty seawater but he did exactly as he was told.

'What, what, what's hap-hap-happening?'

'You jumped off the cliff, Dirk!'

'Why, why'd I do a stupid thing like that?' He sounded just like his old self again.

'Because you thought you could fly, soft lad! And I jumped in to save you.'

'I'm sorry. I'm very, very sorry, Ellie.' His face came over all thoughtful. 'How come I thought I could fly, Ellie?'

'Charlie Chivers and Mrs Nijinsky made you think you could fly.'

'Who? Charlie who? Mrs what?'

'We'll talk about it some other time, Dirk. Just hang on and keep kicking your legs.'

We were drifting along the line of the coast, bobbing on the waves that bounced up and back from the base of the cliffs and the water was so cold I couldn't stop the shaking that made my face wobble and voice rattle.

'Look!' said Dirk, nodding to the bend in the coastline. I turned my head as far as I could to see what he was pointing out and felt like crying with happiness. There was a shelf of rock at the bottom of the cliffs, a place where we could head for, a place above the waterline where we could get out of the sea and shout for help.

I paddled madly with one hand and one arm, kicking like crazy with my legs and feet beneath the water to get us across the water to the shelf.

Above us, in the distance beyond the top of the cliffs, I heard the sound of Dempsey barking, and a voice following him. 'Where? Where? Where are they, Dempsey?' And I couldn't believe my ears at the sound of that voice.

Dempsey's barking grew louder, and again, he asked, 'Where? In the sea, you mean?'

Our sleigh bashed into the side of the shelf, and Dirk scrambled onto the loose shingle and safety. He reached out a hand and, as he dragged me onto the stones, I looked up and saw Dempsey's face poking over the edge above, still barking wildly. And next to Dempsey, Shane Sharples. He looked shocked and called down, 'What are you two doing down there?'

'Sunbathing!' I called back.

'Don't worry,' he cried. 'I'll call the coastguard, I'll save you!'

And with that, Shane disappeared from sight. And Dempsey stopped barking.

I closed my eyes and laughed . . . Shane Sharples to the

rescue . . . And laughed and laughed and laughed.

We're alive, I thought. *We're safe and well and we're alive! Alive! So where does that leave you, Charlie Chivers? And what about you, Mrs Nijinsky?*

Everything went strangely silent, even the sea seemed to hold its breath and hush its tides, as the strangest thing happened. Dirk pointed along the line of the clifftop. Without a whisper of warning, the front end of Mrs Nijinsky's white limousine poked over the edge of the clifftop, then the front wheels, then the body, then the back wheels, and over it went, nosediving into the waters. Down, down, down into the depths of the sea, the almighty crash of metal into water gave way to the noise of the limo being swallowed whole in a single frightening gulp. One moment it was there, the next there was a surge of foam and a mass of huge ripples and then . . . the limo was gone.

I leaned a little way over the side and listened closely. I thought I heard a voice whispering in the sea. Or was it just wave after wave sighing *whoosh*? Or was it Mrs Nijinsky I heard, with her last breath, calling out, 'Dirk and Ellie . . . today of all days . . . when it came to death . . . it was either you . . . or us . . . either you . . . or us . . .'?

Dirk pointed to it. 'Did you? Did you see, see, see *that*?'

'I did, Dirk.'

I stood up and threw the sleigh out to sea, in the direction of the place where the limo had crashed, and watched as it drifted out of our lives forever and into some far-off dark horizon.

Chapter 34

I had a room to myself in the children's wing of Hexhill-on-Sea General Hospital and this meant I got a portable TV set all to myself which was handy for it was the Friday night when 'Where Are They Now?' was due to be screened.

Half an hour before the nightmare TV broadcast began, Dirk and me were sitting nervously on the edge of my bed when the door to my room suddenly burst open and Mum ran in, crying her eyes out and shouting, 'My babies, my babies, oh my poor, poor babies! What has happened to you, my beautiful, darling babies?' She slammed the door shut on the face of the nurse who was trying to calm her down and immediately looked dead worried.

'Oh stop the hoo ha, Mum, and sit down!' I said, as Dirk shoved a chair at her.

'I'm here now, Dirk and Ellie, your loving mum, I'm here, everything's going to be fine. Now tell me everything.'

'No, Mum,' I replied. 'No, no, no. You tell us everything. Like why are you here and where's Dad?'

She'd tried to tone down the punk image and though her hair was still purple it was brushed down and she wasn't wearing half a bathtub of make-up. She looked around the room and said, 'Listen, Dirk, Ellie, you

151

haven't told anyone, have you, about your dad and me . . . you know, about us leaving you on your own?'

She was pulling a sweetie pie face but clearly was very worried about getting into trouble.

'No, Mum,' I told her. 'When they brought us in to hospital and they sent for you and Dad, I said you'd gone away for the day to visit a sick aunt . . . '

She blew a big sigh of relief and muttered, 'Well done, Ellie. And you, Dirk, you didn't tell anyone, did you?'

'What happened, Mum? Why are you back?'

'The tour was a disaster. Your dad's at home, too upset to leave the house. It was an absolute swindle. They expected us to play all night long for next to no money while people threw things at us and your dad got into a fight with this French farmer and had to spend a night in the cells and the places where they put us up were infested with cockroaches and the food wasn't fit for pigs and there was this dreadful man who kept trying to pinch my bottom . . . ' And she went on like this for about twenty minutes and ended up with, 'So when the woman with the tattooed forehead threatened to throw me off the moving train, I said to your dad, I said, *Rodney, that's it! We're going home!*'''

'Home, just in time to see yourself on "Where Are They Now?"' I groaned, dreading what was about to come on TV. 'Making a living disgrace of yourselves.'

'Oh, haven't you heard?' Mum said. 'Your dad was so upset when he found out.'

'Heard what?' asked Dirk.

Just then, a BBC presenter appeared on the screen and spoke these magic words. 'Due to a strike by BBC technicians, we are unable to bring you this week's "Where Are They Now?" And so, instead, here are the highlights of last night's snooker match.'

'Typical, eh?' Mum said.

'Oh, Mum, it's a tragedy...' I lied. I clamped my mouth shut and quietly choked on a spasm of deeply felt laughter.

Just then, another familiar face appeared in the doorway. It was Shane Sharples, carrying a plastic carrier bag.

'Shane? I – you'd better come in,' I said.

'Are you two OK?' he asked, as he walked towards us.

'Thanks,' I replied. 'We're fine. Thanks for, you know, thanks for saving our bacon, Shane.'

He held out the carrier bag to Dirk. It contained a couple of expensive computer magazines and bars of chocolate.

'I've taken Dempsey to our house to mind him. I didn't know where you were, Mrs Beckett.'

Mum smiled falsely and started to blush. I looked at Shane, and wondered if I was dreaming.

'That's very good of you, Shane, thanks very much.'

'I'm glad you're both OK. I'll get going—' He stopped at the door. 'Have you heard the news, Ellie? Dirk?' It must have been obvious from our faces that we hadn't heard any news, but I had a feeling that Shane was about to spill some very serious gravy.

'The coppers sent their frogmen into the sea to fish out the limo and when they did haul it out, all the doors were

153

open. They searched for bodies but they couldn't find any. There was no sign of Mr Chivers or Mrs Nijinsky, just a very expensive and ruined motor car. My dad's got a mate who's a copper and he reckons the car fell off the cliff because the front tyres blew out and the driver lost control on the icy road.'

'Dempsey,' I whispered, remembering how he'd chewed the tyres.

'Dempsey's fine in ours,' said Shane, speaking kindly, trying to make me feel OK about how our dog was doing.

I caught Mum looking at her watch and stifling a yawn.

'Mum,' I said, 'why don't you take Shane home in a taxi?'

She didn't need much more encouragement to get out. She kissed us, and smiled at us, and promised she'd be back in the morning, and promptly got out of our faces.

'Shane!' I called, and he came back. 'Listen, no hard feelings . . .'

'No hard feelings,' he replied, looking a little embarrassed, as he followed Mum out.

Dirk looked hyper-confused. 'Who's Mr Chivers? And Mrs Nijinsky? I think the names ring a bell but—'

'You really can't remember anything about the past twelve days?' I asked him.

He clearly couldn't.

'They're a pair of nobodies,' I told him. 'Some old woman who showed up in school and was never seen again. Don't worry about it, Dirk.'

'I kind of remember something strange,' he said.

'What was that?'

154

'Someone telling me I could fly. I think it was a dream.'

'Yeah, well, dreams aren't real, Dirk, so forget it. You can't fly!'

'I know I can't fly. You fly, you die!'

'Just you remember that next time you feel the urge to throw yourself off the cliffs, Dirk!'

'I won't do that again. No way.'

'Anyway, Dirk, I want you to promise me that. I want you to promise me, you won't try and fly again.'

'I promise you, Ellie, I won't try and fly again.' He went quiet and his face became serious. 'Birds fly,' he said, remembering something very deep down in his memory.

'Go on, Dirk!' I smiled. 'Go on...'

'Birds fly, bats fly, bees fly, butterflies fly, even flies fly... but boys... boys don't fly...'